Written as an allegory, *The Wandering* refutes the humanist belief that man's nature is perfected by the evolutionary process and that mankind can excel through his own efforts. Roger Elwood points to the sole source of humanity's redemption in a provocative space fantasy that will appeal to young people and adults alike.

"Roger Elwood is proving to be the finest modern Christian novelist on the scene today, with more imagination, evangelical dedication, and overall ability than anyone else in a long time. *The Wandering* is the latest proof of this: a superlative novel, richly textured, always surprising in its plot development and possessing such dramatic, emotional, and spiritual power that it should not be missed by anyone who wants to see just where a brilliant author is heading with his work.... Perhaps Roger Elwood's finest accomplishment to date."
    W.S. McBirnie, California Graduate School of Theology

"*The Wandering* is the latest in an expanding group of novels by an author whose works are filled with the kind of spiritual insights that bear comparison with those of C.S. Lewis. *The Wandering*, is fact, may be Elwood's most fascinating work thus far.... Roger Elwood has jumped light-years ahead of the simplistic Christian fiction of a few years ago and may be doing more than any other writer to set a new standard of excellence."
    Harold Lindsell

BY Roger Elwood

Fiction:

Angelwalk
The Christening
The Wandering
Soaring
The Dwellers
The Hitler Syndrome

Nonfiction:

Strange Things Are Happening
Prince of Darkness
People of Destiny
Christian Mothers: Their Joys and Sorrows
The "Innocent" Sins of Everyday Life

The Wandering

Roger Elwood

Power Books
Fleming H. Revell
Old Tappan, New Jersey

Scripture quotations are from the King James Version of the Bible.

Library of Congress Cataloging-in-Publication Data

Elwood, Roger.
   The wandering / Roger Elwood.
     p. cm.
   ISBN 0-8007-5348-8
   I. Title.
  PS3555.L85W36   1990
  813'.54—dc20   89-71341
                                            CIP

Copyright © 1990 by Roger Elwood
Published by the Fleming H. Revell Company
Old Tappan, New Jersey 07675
Printed in the United States of America

Shall I tell you what evil is? To tolerate the things that are called evils, to surrender to them our freedom, in defiance of which we ought to face any suffering.

SENECA
Letters to Lucilius

Acknowledgments

A book the size and scope of *The Wandering* assuredly requires an enormous amount of work, and I have had the real blessing and privilege of some terrific individuals helping me at one point or another, directly or indirectly.

Most crucially, there was my editor, Bill Petersen, an exceptionally gifted chap who happens to stand head and shoulders above virtually all of the editors with whom I have previously worked at secular publishing firms and many of those at Christ-centered companies as well. Bill has the creative sensitivity of an author and the objectivity typical of the very best editors. To work with him is a blessing!

I must also give recognition to Lotus Development Co. for their *Manuscript* computer program—the finest word-processing tool available today, ideally suited for authors. Doing *The Wandering* would have been considerably tougher on a technical level without the features *Manuscript* offers.

Finally, my family and friends have been very supportive: my parents, who share my joyful moments as well as those that are less upbeat; Frank Campana, one of those rarest of true, good friends; Harold Lindsell and Warren Wiersbe, whose insights and reassurances have helped me through the pitfalls; John Long, my newest friend and indeed one of my most valued; and W.S. McBirnie, a gifted and wonderful pastor and author who has never let me down, even when I have been less than diligent myself. They all have been peppered with phone calls arising from a certain condition dubbed "telephonitus" and have endured this with grace and love.

I have probably forgotten a few. If so, let me assure those individuals that their being out of my mind as I compile these acknowledgments in no way means they are out of my heart.

But, really, most of all, I give my thanks, my heart, my very being to Jesus Christ, rescuer of my soul, guardian of my life, and bestower of so many blessings that an acknowledgment many times the length of this one would be grossly insufficient to cover all that He has done for me.

With *Angelwalk*, *The Christening*, and now *The Wandering*, I have made a conscious decision to reveal certain satanic demonic truths. Deception is one of the enemy's most effective weapons. But deception triumphs only insomuch as there is a parallel lack of truth. Therefore, the mission of my books is for them to become weapons that hit Satan as hard and as devastatingly as possible, ripping aside deception and letting the truth that comes from God and God only shine through.

But there is a price to be paid. Satan constantly counterattacks. (If he didn't, he would have ceased being a viable foe a long time ago!) He knows our weaknesses and zeroes in on them, which is why I have felt especially blessed with the kind of fellowship and spiritual integrity manifested by those with whom I've been working. That's a fact, you know. And for the simplest of reasons: It's been needed, much needed.

Prologue

Storyteller was a privileged individual, to be sure. His was the special duty in the midst of the new Heaven and the new Earth of beguiling everyone with reports of the past, in parables and otherwise. He told how God's Master Plan had been fulfilled century after century, if time were any longer the comprehensible device to those awaiting his words, as it had been while they were of bodies corruptible.

"And now we will learn of The Wanderer," Storyteller said, noticing the undisguised and immediate curiosity of those spread out before him on the grassy plain, row after row of the redeemed, their countenances bright and happy indeed.

"Please, the whole story. Every detail, Storyteller," shouted one from the audience.

"Ah, a special individual," he replied, "from eons ago."

And he unrolled some large scrolls of ancient papyrus, his eyes widening as he refreshed himself of the earlier details from the mists of antiquity. He turned directly to the multitudes hanging on his wise and knowing words, and smiled.

"This then is The Wanderer," he told them, his smile broader, as though some special knowledge was yearning to break out of the cocoon of himself and be born right before their eyes, but it was not quite time. Yet the surety of their reactions when they finally did know bemused him.

"We will begin somewhere in space, out beyond the earth of yesterday."

And thus Storyteller grabbed their attention and held it for some small part of eternity as he sat atop a small hill, a gentle wind whispering out of the east to play momentarily with the edges of the scroll. No one spoke a syllable, hushed into the silence of awe as the epic tale began.

Part One

When men are ruled by fear, they strive to prevent the very changes that will abate it.

ALAN PATON

1

The nightmare was familiar. It had invaded Neshi's sleeptime often over the years, persistently wrapping itself around him until a subconscious defense mechanism wrenched him awake, saturated in perspiration, the nerves over all his body rebelling. Sometimes he would be crying; sometimes no emotions came at all, his reservoir of these spent on the nightmare, with little left over, except perhaps that of fear, dark, chilling, and yet not so beyond reason that it could be conveniently scoffed at and then discarded, leaving no imprint. . . .

Neshi stood at the gate to a city with a wall around it thrice his height. As he approached, he could detect the odors immediately, sickening bits and pieces of scents merged together by the breezes on which they were carried. Surely he could turn back and not have to discover the conditions that gave the odors birth, for if they were but mere hints diluted by the air and the passage of whatever time had elapsed before he detected them, then what must they be in reality?

The gate swung open slowly. Neshi saw a maze of winding narrow streets surrounded by buildings that made them rather like unnatural canyons fashioned by hand—not by the eons granted to nature's work in the normal course of things—the ground of ancient cobblestone, piles of manure here and there, thin clouds of dust hanging in the air, a curtain of fluctuating density.

At first there were no sounds, just those invisibly swirling thick scents. He had never been in such a soundless place before. His society was always filled with some kind of sound. He could not escape it if he wanted to; peace and quiet was not in his vocabulary. There were sounds from the view-tubes, sounds of the flight machines, sounds of others of his kind talking—sounds of every intensity and a myriad of origins. There could be no quiet, it was decreed. Only the grave was quiet, and thoughts of death were forbidden. But, as Neshi walked forward, unknowing of his destination, down one of the streets, this unaccustomed quiet evaporated, and he heard a thin buzzing—faint, hardly discernible, then finally louder.

A body was lying in a doorway of one of the buildings. Whoever it had been was dead. Flies were feasting. He pulled back, disgusted. The body's mouth was open, frozen in a cry of agony. From directly inside the building he could hear slurping sounds, low voices, and a hint of weeping.

He walked away from that spot, not wanting to see what was inside, not wanting to imagine.

Approaching a square at the center of the city, Neshi

came upon a crowd. There were little fires at different spots, and those in the crowd were gathered around one or the other, partly against the cold, partly to wait for the food that was being cooked. Raw pieces of pale meat with red streaks turned darker as the flames cooked it before it was handed to the hungry who consumed this food without being satisfied and grabbed for more, risking even the flame as they tore it off the spits, hands shaking, mouths dripping foamy drool.

They detected his presence and turned toward him, all of them, their faces shrunken, bony.

"We must survive. The city is surrounded. We have nothing but each other for companionship, comfort, and food."

Neshi ran down another street, a street, like the others, littered with the dead and the dying. Everywhere he went, there were bodies. Everywhere the living feasted so perversely.

Those alive saw the intruder and chased him.

But I am not dead! Why go you after me? Why reach out with your skeletal arms and your unholy tongues seeking forbidden tastes from streets turned tombs, laid out before you like legless tables at a grotesque buffet, your teeth red with blood? Finally he was back at the gate. It started to swing open, and he sighed with relief as he walked outside, only to cry in agony as an enemy spear entered his chest.

And in the wind perhaps there were words, but he was never sure from where, the wind nothing more than a frenzied guess, and always the thought that it was only the encompassing tinges of madness and in fact he had heard nothing but his own death rattle mocking him, but always the same as he died, and the sounds—phantom or real or whatever—nevertheless washed over him like a noxious blanket until the sun was no more and the city was gone and the enemy, bored with its singular kill, went through the gate to add to the infamy with gloating anticipation.

The sounds, whispering yet insistent, forming words that would haunt him well into the following day. . . .

Jerusalem, Jerusalem, how I weep for thee.

2

A couple of years before, Neshi had approached his profession with considerably more zest. As a Tech Detective, he was paid well, lived a fairly adventurous albeit dangerous life, and was a number of notches up the ladder in his society.

Tech Detectives were a crack unit set up decades earlier to handle crimes beyond the ordinary: tracking down a mass murderer, for example. They also worked with cases outside the jurisdiction of the cities, such as the outlaw bands. Tekkies, as they came to be nicknamed, wore uniforms with a distinctive emblem on the front, essentially a stylized rendering of a computer, symbolic of the fact that they used all the latest technological devices. They had far fewer restrictions on their travels than other citizens, and they carried a rather romantic image in the minds of the public.

But more than anything in his career, a calamity proved to be a profound turning point in his life.

Etarina, his wife.

She was out walking with a friend one evening. Both were approached by one of the gangs that generally kept to the city's fringes near the surrounding wastelands called the moors and seldom ventured into what was considered the safe interior. But this band of five proved bolder than the others.

Etarina and the other female were raped and then murdered. Their bodies were discovered by a neighborhood patrol-male who immediately contacted Neshi on his re-mobeep unit, a special beeper with an effective range many times that of the commercially available models.

Neshi then had the task that every citizen of his world was legally obliged to carry out: arranging for Etarina to be taken to the nearest Trans Unit for disposal. The planet was largely inhospitable, the reclaimed land areas quite small in comparison to its overall size. Overcrowding was a persistent problem. Thus, no space could be allocated for burial areas. The best way to proceed, the government felt, was to use the organs and limbs of the deceased for medical experiments and transplantation.

The rate of transplantations grew rapidly over the years. As for those bodies badly damaged and not otherwise useful, the bone marrow and peripheral blood cells were implanted into animals in an attempt to use the creatures as breeding chambers for the production of various cells. The rejection problem was dealt with by radiation that rendered the animal tissue unable to reject the foreign substances, which were kept implanted for up to ten days. That limitation was necessary because the amount of radiation demanded would kill a creature within ten days.

In a world of limited resources, this breeding of various cells proved indispensable.

From the moment her body was picked up, Etarina was literally out of his hands, part of the recycling routine. Any attempt to deviate would have been illegal.

Knowing that he would never see her again, he stayed with the two blood-drenched bodies until a Trans Unit team was dispatched.

The look of pain frozen on her face would haunt him for a very long time. Passersby stopped and tried to console him. In a society in which any thought of an afterlife was quite nebulous, with no clear destination for the soul when all physical signs of life ceased, death was not taken lightly. Flesh-and-blood life was something real and absolute that his kind could literally touch and hold, not the formless suppositions of ethereal spirit.

They had been married less than a year. What made matters especially tragic was the fact that she was also pregnant.

Hours later, Neshi had taken off his Tech Detective uniform and put on sleep clothes, but he could not submit to sleeptime oblivion as yet, consumed as he was with thoughts of the night before, when she was beside him.

"Etarina, my love," he had whispered into her ear.

"Baba, my love, my husband, the father of my child," she had replied, using the nickname she had given him because of his tendency to talk too much, even as they were getting ready to make love.

He spoke her name that following night—cringing when there was no voice, soft and gentle, to say "Baba" in return—but could not do so again for many months, though she was in his thoughts and his dreams unceasingly.

There was no grave to visit, no place to stand and ponder what could never be retrieved. Death was a terrible intrusion, its residue done away with as quickly as possible. Only life mattered, for that was all Neshi and his kind had. Any existence subsequent to death, about which they mused in idle moments, seemed boring, devoid of personality.

Two years had gone by since that terrible night. The passage of time had eased his sorrow, but it also took the joy from his life. He had moved from their apartment into a smaller one, leaving behind countless pieces of furniture and much else that reminded him of Etarina.

And he had tried to get on with his job, keeping his pain to himself as it loosened its grip day by day. Then one day he was asked to investigate the so-called hunchback murders.

The cities spotted around the planet were constantly besieged by roving bandits from the moors and beyond, outlaws refusing to submit to the social order of a world government that controlled every aspect of its citizens' existence. The longer they refused offers of reconciliation, the more their numbers grew, as males and females reproduced in harsh places of habitation, which seemed to everyone in the cities to be utterly stupid when they could have the best possible conditions simply by agreeing to live the way the majority were living, and in reasonable happiness.

But the hunchback murders proved quite different from the crimes of the bandits, in part because of their frequency and their ferocity, yet mostly due to the murderer himself, a creature hunched over in a permanently threatening stance that would have seemed terrible without his having committed a single crime.

Those victims who lived long enough to describe him painted a bizarre picture of their assailant: the hunchbacked shape; the thin and bony face with pronounced cheeks, jutting jaw, and very large eyes; across the very top of his forehead, a rather wide scar.

He would shout at them, his tone thickly gutteral, the words unintelligible. Actually a rather slight figure, he was surprisingly agile and able to catch any of the victims who tried to flee.

All were females, except in one instance where a male passerby tried to help and had his stomach ripped open as a result.

All were females.

Neshi tried to fathom that. No other case to which he had been assigned over the years had been weighted toward one sex or the other.

After having studied these deaths, shrouded as they were in such mystery, Neshi agreed to take the assignment.

Within twenty-four hours, he was front-page news. Something of a celebrity already because of his other exploits, Neshi became the most publicized of all the elite Tech Detectives. Under ordinary circumstances, this additional recognition would have made him an object of intense jealousy at Tech Headquarters.

Not this time.

The hunchback murders had sent tendrils of alarm into every sector of society. Who was this creature? How could he so persistently elude capture? Where was his base of operations?

And there was a subsidiary danger that none of the

media mentioned because government officials had placed them under the severest of restrictions: Would the hunchback become a kind of symbol to all the outlaw groups nibbling at the fringes of each of the cities? Would he generate an "If he can do it, so can we" syndrome that would encourage them to step up their antigovernment activities?

The potential of that scenario made it necessary for the government to offer the public a countervailing symbol of their own—and that was where Neshi's publicity came into the picture.

Tech Headquarters was a five-story metal and smoked glass building in the geometric center of the city. On a clear day, the intense sunlight bounced off its exterior so blindingly that looking at it for more than a second or two was blinding.

The efficiency mentality of the Tech Detectives Division of Government Law Enforcement was manifested in the precise orderliness that was apparent from the instant anyone set foot inside its headquarters. Frivolity was forbidden; every second of each working day had to breed accomplishment. *Slothfulness* was not a word in the vocabulary of anyone who worked for the division, whether they were Tech Detectives or support personnel such as secretaries, errand boys, or others.

Every floor seemed dominated by computers, one on each desk, all of them linked with the government's mainframe. Even the guard on the ground floor had one.

As Neshi walked down the hallway to the main suite of offices on the third floor, he noticed none of the usual activity. His intuition kicked up a warning signal.

Once inside, as he said hello, the receptionist looked up

at him, smiled, blushed, and conspicuously busied herself with a pile of papers on top of her desk.

Beyond the reception room was a large area of open offices. Some of the rookie Tech Detectives occupied these, along with researchers and other personnel. Neshi had earned the privilege of a small enclosed office at the north end.

Suddenly, everyone stood up.

"Yes?" he said, not sure of what was going on.

Then he saw someone he never expected to see: Mayor Gursack, probably the most aloof political figure in decades, extending his hand in greeting.

"Neshi, Neshi!" the mayor exclaimed.

And everyone began singing the Tech Detective theme song.

In the course of a few more minutes, Neshi had been praised by the mayor and applauded by all those present. Then the mayor asked him into the conference room, where the mood turned serious.

"My friend," Gursack said, "I wanted to talk with you one-on-one, with no cameras around, no eavesdroppers of any kind—you and me only. Are you comfortable with this?"

Neshi nodded that he was.

"Sit down, please," Gursack said as he took a place at the long polished nukecki wood table.

"This hunchback murder business is really more critical than most people realize," Gursack began. "We have been telling our folks that they are being protected from those gangs of bandits and the rest of their ilk. Oh, the fact that we need as many Tech Detectives as we have presently implies that crime is hardly licked, but I suggest there's a difference between, shall we say, 'normal' crimes of passion and robberies and those crimes that are seditious in nature. The commission of a rape, for example, is regrettable indeed, but it takes on a lesser significance, if we were to be quite straightforward, than a group of traitors attacking a power plant in an effort to diminish the capacity of this society to function. Especially when their avowed intention is to take over.

"Tech Detectives have been shifted with well-modulated deliberateness over to the seditionary crimes, as you know, and the burden of so-called 'everyday crimes' gradually put in the hands of the regular law enforcement officials. Even this could tip off citizens that something is going on. That is why the media have not mentioned the shift."

When the mayor paused, Neshi answered, "And you want to make a big thing of my involvement in the hunchback case because it creates the illusion that no such shift has been occurring, that these murders are obviously not the work of the roving bandits but of a single individual who is quite deranged."

"Exactly, Neshi. Exactly!" Gursack said, his large frame shaking much like a bowl of pudding.

"I was happy to volunteer, sir, without knowing what you have just mentioned."

"Good! It will mean, at times, a bit less privacy than you are accustomed to enjoying, the media being what they are."

"A dichotomy then?"

"Pardon me, Neshi?"

"I must pursue a highly intensive investigation in as much secrecy as possible while making sure the media believe they are being fully informed."

"Difficult, I admit."

"But with the support of the mayor," Neshi added, a knowing twinkle in his eyes, "I am sure we can count on success."

"We *must*, Neshi, or else this could get out of hand."

The pregnant tone of his voice and the look on his face carried more conviction than was customary with this particular politician.

3

The kind of cooperation Neshi was being accorded meant that he had to perform. He usually came through well enough, but this time the pressure was enhanced. If he didn't accomplish what he was supposed to do, it would be a major embarrassment to Tech Detective Headquarters, and he could hardly escape the fallout.

Practically all the Tech Detectives were placed under his direct control. Not even the mayor expected him to track down the hunchback single-handedly. He made sure every area of the city was covered, reserving just one for himself.

"I have a hunch about Old Town," he told a fellow Tech Detective named Turnish as they sat in a tavern two blocks from TDH.

"It's because of The Dome, right?" Turnish said, a knowing smile on his face.

"How did you guess?" Neshi replied sarcastically. "Does *everyone* know what I think of the games?"

"Everyone," Turnish assured him.

"But isn't it obvious?"

"That the center of sanctioned violence might become a breeding place for violence that threatens the faith of our citizens in the very government giving them a once-a-week dose of it?"

"You have to admit the notion carries with it a certain beguiling irony."

"Brilliant supposition," Turnish remarked. "I guess I'm a little jealous."

"Jealous?"

"Because I didn't think of it myself."

They clicked their mugs together and swilled down the rest of their fermented kirlici juice.

Less than a week after he had been given the assignment, Neshi decided to follow his intuition, a kind of sixth sense that prodded him incessantly and was enhanced when the files confirmed that several of the murders occurred at night, the majority of these within walking distance of The Dome.

Neshi ran over that neighborhood in his mind as he washed and dressed for an evening of walking around, asking questions, seeing what he could uncover. Old Town was a section of the city that was, to put it mildly, less advanced than others, though not a slum by any means. To describe it as old-fashioned was appropriate, the buildings primarily made of wood instead of the steel and glass used elsewhere. Since the architecture was from another era, the materials no longer being used in a similar manner, the quaintness of Old Town made it quite a tourist attraction for citizens from other cities on the planet.

Neshi had investigated two previous murders in Old Town several years before. He was impressed by the place and saw its mostly elderly citizens as a curious analogy for Old Town itself. They were nearing the end of their lives. When they were dead, their bodies would be cut apart and shipped to nearby Trans Units. Someday Old Town itself would go. Its mostly one- and two-story buildings rested on exceptionally valuable real estate. Tall apartments and office buildings could serve vastly more citizens in the same amount of space.

Neshi remembered the odors drifting through the air as Etarina and he once took a walk through Old Town. The rest of the city was more impersonal; Old Town was the only surviving neighborhood with any individuality.

"I feel life here more," Etarina had remarked.

Neshi had nodded.

"We go to work, earn our money, return to our apartments, and that is it," she added. "Here, there is much more—"

"Sharing?"

"Yes, sharing."

They could see elderly couples sitting on porches, wash hanging out on clotheslines. The sounds of conversation were carried on gentle night breezes.

Ahead, towering over the old buildings, was The Dome.

Etarina shivered as they turned and walked in another direction, away from The Dome. "A monument to madness," she said, pulling her jacket tightly around her.

"And death," Neshi added.

She put her arm around him and hugged him closer. "Have you seen the games?" she asked.

"I have."

"Aren't they really quite awful?"

"But sanctioned by the government, don't forget."

"That doesn't guarantee their morality, their decency."

"But it does portend their continuance."

They approached one of the few Temples of Thought and Spirit[1] in their city, the only one in Old Town. Like the other buildings, it manifested the more ornate architectural patterns of an earlier time.

"Shall we go inside?" Neshi had asked.

"Why not?" Etarina agreed.

Stained-glass windows portrayed scenes of innocuous bliss, citizens with happy faces, some surrounded by cottony clouds, others playing in green fields with snow-capped mountains in the distance. One pane was more somber. Someone was obviously on her deathbed with her relatives gathered around, and the dying citizen's soul

---

[1]The Thought and Spirit movement had been around for centuries, so long in fact that its exact origins could not be ascertained, as the availability and the accuracy of records became less "predictable" the further into the past researchers went. It was a view of life and death that became less compelling as his race's scientific and other "here and now" achievements gained momentum. In times past when there was much mystery about their world, Neshi's kind felt drawn to expectations that gave them less concern about the future. But as they took more control, as they gained more relevant insights, any devotion to the Thought and Spirit theology weakened until it was a negligible factor in the lives of a handful of citizens.

The difficulty was that Thought and Spirit had no hard core. It was based upon formless notions about what happened after death claimed the physical body. It had not been forged in the furnace of any contest between good and evil. There was no god, no devil, just a kind of institutionalized wishful thinking. Emotion ruled. If citizens felt good, that was a barometer of their success in implementing Thought and Spirit; if they were depressed, that meant they were out of fellowship with what were called the Currents of the Cosmos.

was leaving her body, to be melded in with a sky comprised of countless faces, all with blissful expressions.

"The Currents of the Cosmos," Neshi sighed wearily.

"But it is better than nothing," Etarina interjected. "To think that we cease to exist when we die is quite terrifying. But to look forward to joy unending—how wonderful."

"I have never been able to escape the suspicion that we are missing a hugely important part of the picture, though. Is this all, Etarina? A choice between the scientific and materialistic obsessions of our age and the vaporousness of Thought and Spirit?"

"The original settlers were a terrified lot, it is said. Can you blame them for devising thought patterns that would enable them to cope with the harshness of their lives?"

"But isn't there anything more substantial than what we make up, Etarina? How real can the so-called verities of Thought and Spirit be? Have we nothing more than the conjectures of those who sought to insulate themselves from the harsh realities around them? Thought and Spirit has come to seem less expedient as life has—"

"Shush," she said. "I don't want my husband to feel that he has to fulfill his nickname all the time."

They sat down on one of the long seats in the temple.

The designers had attempted to inject an illusion of warmth and naturalness, with wood in abundance on the walls and floor. The ceiling was cathedral in style, with thick beams leading to the pinnacle.

"We aren't supposed to do much thinking here," Neshi whispered sarcastically. "Just sit and stare."

The atmosphere was conducive to a sense of mindlessness, the piped-in music helping to set the mood, the odors of incense lulling one.

A Guide, as he was called, approached the two of them a short while later.

"Happy to see you here," he said, smiling ear to ear.

"But you don't even know us," Neshi said, despite Etarina's tug at the sleeve of his garment.

"The Cosmos is filled with those who were once strangers."

"How do you *know* that? Have you seen any evidence to support your beliefs?"

"Faith is the essence of hope."

"But what about reality?" Neshi added. "You are preaching a formless eternal nothingness."

"Happiness is what is."

Neshi took a songbook from a holder in the back of the seat in front of him. "This I can hold."

"But it is *only* that. Happiness is within."

"But happiness based upon delusion is idle fantasy. The real world dooms it."

"After you have shed that body of yours, fantasy will be the new reality. After you have shed that body of yours, after you have—"

The Guide was standing there, sputtering, repeating the same words over and over, jumbling them.

Etarina and Neshi stood, backing away from him.

Sparks started to come out of the Guide's ears. Grease seeped from his eyes like strange tears.

"An android!" Etarina exclaimed.

"And not even serviced properly," Neshi noticed.

Once outside, they turned and looked at the old temple.

"None of it is real," Etarina said.

"He was repeating what they fed into him. He believed none of it because machines are incapable of beliefs. And the Thought and Spirit hierarchy place so little credence in their own precepts that they feel a mechanical thing can do just as good a job as any of them!"

"He talked of joy, of happiness," Etarina added, her tone depressed. "What can an android know of any of that?"

They hugged each other then.

"This is all there is, really," he whispered. "What you and I share, *that's* real."

A few weeks later, Etarina was dead, a victim of the violence that the games in Old Town were supposed to alleviate.

4

Neshi had no interest in attending the games regularly. After years as a Tech Detective, he had seen more bloodshed than most on his world would ever witness in a lifetime of gladiatorial competition. Of course what he encountered was devoid of the glitz, the hype bestowed upon the weekly event by a government eager to offer the populace outlets for their frustrations so they would not otherwise overflow in more destructive manifestations such as outright sedition.

But that night, long-nurtured intuition motivated him to take a seat inside. As a Tech Detective, he had his pick of free seats. As he sat in one of the most prized locations in the entire arena watching the first battle, he could only marvel at how the bureaucracy had messed up a society that was once exceptionally promising. Now it was a society of ideals gone sour, its former impetus to be the best, the most moral, the most inventive and advanced group of beings in the entire galaxy submerged in the excrement of its increasingly ignoble deeds. Government spotted these trends, but rather than offer a collective beacon of decency, a lighthouse drawing those afloat on uncertain seas to a safe haven, politicians catered to the corruption by giving citizens what they wanted, even if that ultimately proved to be a malignancy that would spread wider and further, without ever abating.

How I weep. . . .

Three words from his nightmare pushed into his consciousness. Neshi shivered for a second or two, then managed to temporarily wipe them from his mind.

The arena itself was certainly an architectural phenomenon, even in a society accustomed to a surfeit of daring designs. Neshi, during the course of his rare visits, always marveled at the sweep and majesty of the building around him.

Such money spent on a monument to a bankrupt philosophy, he thought to himself. *For the thousands inside, this is a once-a-week gratification of carnal desires. And yet there are so many in the bureaucracy and the media, in civic and other organizations, so many hypocritically professing outrage and alarm at the incidence of crime throughout the inhabited sectors of this world.*

The arena was essentially a dome made of crystals taken from nearby mines. Other materials could have been used, but it was claimed that crystals in some mysterious way contributed to the mood within The Dome, fostering a ravenous psychic atmosphere of bloodlust from which participants would emerge temporarily satiated until their next weekly indulgence.

Neshi had been there the day The Dome was dedicated.

He had stood in its very center, looking up at the crystals supported by round metal girders. Closing his eyes briefly, he could feel something tugging at him, as though trying to reach inside his very being. At first he decided it was merely the power of suggestion. A great deal of publicity had been generated about the so-called mystical powers inherent in the crystals. He had scoffed at these prior to that first day in The Dome, but not since then, and especially not in view of the tumult that arose when the games were held there. Conceivably the citizens would have gone "over the edge" in any event, but he nonetheless sensed that the crystals magnified their reactions to the point of the maniacal.

Crystalmania was everywhere, not just under The Dome laden with them. In some shape or form, they were in virtually every residence as decorations; in player machines that offered laserized sonic reproduction; cooking appliances; timepieces of precise accuracy; or as a part of some ritual of healing or "joining," as it was called. Apart from this, and perhaps most tellingly of all, they were starting to show up in government offices. He had seen officials rubbing smooth, oblong-shaped crystals before making critical decisions that would affect life everywhere on the planet.

I weep. . . .

He brushed those vagrant words out of his mind as he turned to concentrate on the contest directly in front of him.

One gladiator was always flesh and blood, usually a criminal convicted of more than a middling transgression against the law. His opponent was anything but flesh and blood: Android.

Outwardly they seemed quite real, with quite astonishingly lifelike faces, but inside they were flashing lights and plastic tubing and copper wires and computer memory chips and more.

The winner of the contest was always the android. For strength, dexterity, and overall logic, androids had no equal. The result, routinely, was death for the criminal. And it was a brutally painful death, with the victim lingering for a minute or two. The whole idea was to make this part of the contest as spectacular and satisfying for the crowd as possible.

The criminal was furnished with a metal club with long spikes at one end. The android had built-in lasers, darts that could be expelled without warning, and a supply of nerve gas that caused temporary paralysis. Death for the criminal usually involved being zapped by the gas and then opened up from neck to lower torso by a laser cut. He would plead to the crowd for mercy, but mercy was never bestowed.

Neshi settled down in his seat, separated from the contest by a force field of impenetrable energy that cast a heatlike shimmer around the circumference of the arena so the criminals could not escape before the outcome was otherwise decided. He had seen enough of these to be bored on the one hand and increasingly disturbed on the other. Not a single android had ever been bested, and not a single crowd had ever taken pity upon the loser. The only suspense that remained was in how long it took the criminal to die. And that was the main ingredient in a betting system that added a further note of corruption to the proceedings. Each seat in The Dome was equipped with a small box, inside of which was a miniaturized computer electronically joined to a huge computer in an underground room directly beneath the arena. Bets were transmitted by the pressing of the appropriate keys, together with the proper identification code, which was given to each citizen at birth.

This particular contest started in a fashion more or less identical to countless others over the years. Android and criminal were announced at the outset.

"Number 235XT will confront Zgin Parsin in two minutes and five seconds!"

The announcer's voice was then replaced by music that built to a deafening pitch as the contestants came out into the arena from opposite sections of the field.

Zgin Parsin was uncommonly hefty, taller than the average criminal, broader, more toned in his musculature, with a finely chiseled bone structure evident in his face. He also seemed more confident than others Neshi had seen. Wearing the usual strip of cloth around his middle, he made an impressive appearance.

Yet the android to oppose him seemed even more substantial than most of the others, probably weighing in at a third of a ton or more. It was roughly Parsin's height but much broader, and it undoubtedly had the customary bag of tricks.

"Let the contest begin!"

Parsin was obviously prepared. Number 235XT started to raise its arm to shoot a dart from a hole at the end of its thumb. The criminal threw the spiked club directly at his opponent's hand, managing to hit the thumb head-on, ripping it from its socket.

Number 235XT seemed stunned but realized that the criminal was left with no real weapon. Something resembling a human smile crossed its face. It spread its legs wide, in the war-cry stance common to its model year, and prepared to fire a laser burst from tubes in its chest.

Parsin simply dove partway between those huge legs,

grabbed the club, and scrambled to his feet as he swung the weapon at 235XT's abdominal area—all with such speed that the crowd let out a collective gasp of surprise.

The android tottered but didn't fall. Parsin hit it again and again, on the legs, at the shoulders, but still it stood, though severely damaged. The criminal swung once too often and 235XT grabbed his wrist, lifted him up, and threw him to the left, where Parsin landed with a painful thump.

Then 235XT took its opponent by the neck, hoisted him up, and held him in midair. The crowd sensed that a kill might be close. Shouts of "Death! Death! Death to the criminal!" spread, rising in decibel level.

Parsin groped into a side pocket of his garb and pulled out a thin transparent tube, quickly emptying its oily contents on his neck and the android's hand. Seconds later he slid from its grasp.

The crowd roared with appreciation.

But Parsin was obviously hurt, choking, spitting up blood, hardly able to stand. And then suddenly he did something unexpected. He just stood there, stock-still, facing 235XT. Even the android appeared puzzled that its opponent seemed to be inviting the next attack although he had nothing with which to defend himself.

Android 235XT ran straight at Zgin Parsin. If it had collided with the criminal, every bone in Parsin's body would have been broken. Androids seemed fleshy on the outside, but they had a frame of hard metal, and they could run with the speed of a racing vehicle.

Only a few feet separated them. Parsin was immobile, as though prepared for his doom and accepting it.

Less than a yard. . . .

Parsin simply stepped aside. By that time the android

had built up such momentum that it went speeding past him, right into the force field!

Sparks blew out from 235XT's infrastructure, bursts of flame as well, followed by thin reeds of smoke. No words escaped its lips; it died in eerie silence, belying its flesh-and-blood look.

And in dying it took the force field with it, setting up an electronic chain reaction throughout The Dome. Laserlike bursts of light bounced off the crystals and back into the crowd. Panic reigned as citizens died by the scores, their bodies cut up or filled with raw, unmodulated energy and then exploding like helium-filled balloons.

Neshi jumped into the arena, heading for the gladiators' entrance. He had to cross Zgin Parsin's path to do so.

"You!" the criminal said. "The finest of all the Tech Detectives!"

Neshi ignored those words as he tried to push him to one side.

But even though greatly weakened, Parsin had unsuspected strength, and he grabbed Neshi around the neck. "Listen. Please, you must *hear* what I have to say!"

Neshi had fought many such encounters over the years; Parsin was no match for him at that point. Neshi threw the criminal's enormous bulk into the air and over his shoulder with a single, well-conditioned move, then he proceeded toward the exit again.

"Remember Jerusalem!"

Neshi stopped instantly. He hurried to Parsin's body, bending over him, gently lifting him up. "You mention Jerusalem. How do you know that name?"

"Because . . . we . . . are like it. We all have descended into the same . . . pit . . . of . . . evil as the forces of destruction gather around us."

Neshi scoffed at the idea. "We are strong. We can survive for eternity."

Parsin grabbed his collar, a look of urgency on his scarred face. "Soon it will all be ended. Many like me will rise and sow the seeds of death."

Neshi's impatience was fed by the heightened sounds of chaos around him. "I'm going now. This is no time for your ravings."

"But *you* are to survive. With you there can be some hope. But not on this world. Not here."

And with that, Zgin Parsin was dead.

Neshi laid the body on the floor of the arena and stood, his eyes taking in the sights before him: multicolored beams of light bouncing from crystal to crystal and then being zapped down into the crowd; screams filling the air; citizen pushing citizen aside; others being trampled in the midst of mass panic.

How I weep. . . .

The sense of those words, the implicit tragedy in them, overwhelmed him, and he ran from The Dome into the cool night air, his body once again filled with the chill of his oft-repeated nightmare.

5

Within just two hours, The Dome was a skeletal shell of its former hedonistic glory. Most of its crystals were lying in the shattered ruins in front of Neshi; a few hung loosely from what was left of the frame of The Dome. Neshi picked one up, examined it briefly, then tossed it back. An odor of death hung about the site, and there were the sounds of chaos—sirens piercing the stillness of the night, cries, shouts, vehicles racing away with the injured.

A hand dropped on his shoulder and startled Neshi. He turned suddenly. "Ferene!" he exclaimed.

Ferene was a longtime friend from TDH, a squatty little individual, but friendly and exceptionally gifted. "Neshi, Neshi. Why is it that you almost always find yourself in the midst of a mess?" Ferene commented in sardonic fashion.

Neshi shrugged his shoulders, unable to provide an answer.

"What happened, my friend?" Ferene asked.

Neshi told him everything. "Again that word, *Jerusalem*. What can it mean? Such a strange word."

"That it is, my friend. Strange indeed." Ferene shivered a bit despite himself.

"Is there something else?"Neshi asked, aware that this was not typical of Ferene, who had previously given the impression that nothing could ever unnerve him.

Ferene looked directly at Neshi and smiled slightly. "As observant as ever! Yes, there is something. Talk of an upcoming mass attack by the bandits."

"What?"

"Exactly my reaction when I heard about it. If they are such a low-life band of amateurs, then their planning an attack must mean that they are also mentally unbalanced and can be easily disposed of. Or that they are stronger and smarter than we've been giving them credit for."

"Any idea of when the attack will come?"

"Not anything specific. No date that can be pinpointed. Just sometime during this planetary season." Ferene cleared his throat and added, "My friend, there's something else. I happened to be in the computer center the other day and found this on the floor." Ferene took a thin strip of plastic computer tape out of his pocket and showed it to Neshi.

"Have you played it?"

"Yes."

"What are the contents?"

"Take it back to your place. Put it into your compuview unit. Let me know what you think."

"Can't you tell me now?"

"I want to see if you react the way I did."

Neshi nodded in agreement. Ferene was indeed acting uncharacteristically.

They shook hands and left each other.

Neshi slipped the film into a pocket of his outer garment and walked around Old Town. The nights tended to be quite cool. All the citizens wore heavy clothes, thick and warm but somewhat cumbersome. But a Tech Detective had to be able to move quickly, unhampered by bulky clothing, so his outer garment was designed of synthetic materials developed to provide insulation without much weight. It was comprised of three wafer-thin layers, the most important one being the middle layer, a foam-type substance that absorbed and amplified body heat.

Already the trauma of being in The Dome was wearing off, one of the advantages of intensive Tech Detective training which, in addition to being physical, was also psychological, training the mind and emotions to achieve the same kind of resiliency as the body. If not for that training, Neshi might well have joined Etarina in death by his own hand.

The citizens of Old Town were friendly. Some sitting on their porches called out to him to offer a beverage or some confection. He smiled and told them that he was in the midst of an investigation and had to hurry.

An elderly male walked up to him and wished him success. "That hunchback thing, whatever it is, has been around here recently. We're very scared, all of us."

"Recently?" Neshi asked.

"Just a couple of nights ago."

"But no murder or disappearance was reported then."

"He doesn't always kill."

"What is your name, sir?"

"Daniek."

"Daniek, what *does* he do?"

"He slinks in and out of the alleyways and down the side streets, muttering something to himself. We can never understand him, though it sounds like the same word each time."

"Tracking another victim?"

"I think it is more than that, Tech Detective Neshi." Daniek's eyes widened as he remembered something. "Would you wait just a moment, please?"

Neshi nodded.

Daniek went back into his residence and emerged with a tattered, dirt-streaked sheet of paper. "I can't decipher what is written on it. Can you?"

Neshi looked at the scrawl. "His hand must have been shaking as he wrote it." Water had also splashed on the paper, obscuring the writing further.

"I brought this up because, well, he has written other notes and left them behind," Daniek recalled. "But none of the messages have been in better shape."

"How often, would you say?"

"Too often to count."

Neshi asked him why none of this had been reported.

"Oh, the mayor was told when he came through, trying to make himself look good."

"Gursack knew?"

"He did." Daniek paused briefly. "Tech Detective Neshi, may I venture a guess about the hunchback?"

"Certainly."

"I think he's trying to contact someone."

"What brings you to that?"

"I was almost a Tech Detective myself."

"Yes?"

"Well, that *is* a slight exaggeration. I trained to be one, but I couldn't stand the strain. I wasn't up to the physical endurance required. But I do remember how we were taught to find the trail of a fugitive by looking for footprints in the mud, by examining bushes for torn clothing—you remember it well, I suppose."

"I do, very well, Daniek."

"There was one fugitive, apparently, who wanted to be caught. But he directed his planted clues to one particular Tech Detective whom he had learned about through the media. He convinced himself that only that one was worthy."

"As in that case, you think these scrawled notes, whatever they happen to say, are being deliberately left by the hunchback?"

"Yes, I do."

"Very interesting. I thank you for your insights."

Daniek beamed from ear to ear. Neshi said good-bye and continued on his way.

Finally he decided to visit the spot where the last hunchback murder had taken place. It was in an alley between two residential buildings that were three stories tall and wood framed. The odor of age was quite strong, musty from decades of dampness and unavoidable deterioration. There was no paving, and he found one tiny section where blood had coalesced the dirt into little mounds of now dried mud. Light from inside the buildings illuminated the alley to a respectable level of visibility.

Could the murderer have come from one of the apartments overlooking the spot?

The alley wasn't a dead end; it continued on between buildings on the next street. Neshi walked its full length and initially found nothing. Then he saw a pile of rocks to one side and a small object partially buried among them. He bent down and pried it loose.

A plastic tube, not much larger than an ordinary writing instrument.

He looked at it curiously. Both ends were sealed. The tube itself was transparent; he could see two sections inside, one holding some kind of yellow liquid, the other filled with a green substance.

The tube was flexible. He could bend it slightly. As he did, something quite remarkable occurred: the tube lit up with astonishing brightness as the two colors mixed, a light coming from within that was far more vivid than he could possibly have imagined.

Startled, he dropped the tube. One end split open, and some of the fluid spilled out, forming an illuminated puddle on the dirt.

Neshi grabbed the tube and tilted the broken end upward so that no more fluid would be lost. Then he took out his portacall[2] unit and asked for a lab tech immediately. Within twenty-five minutes, an individual named Cortuk had arrived.

"What in the—" the tech said.

"It's been fading a bit," Neshi said. "The portion on the ground faded more than what's in the tube."

"How bright was it at the outset?"

"Very."

Both suspected radioactivity at first, but a reading on a detectometer that Cortuk had brought with him as a precaution indicated none. This provided an absolutely accurate measurement of radioactivity, and its tiny com-

[2] This was a portable miniaturized shortwave unit that, despite a size that enabled it to fit into the palm of the user's hand, had a range of ten miles or more—required equipment for all Tech Detectives.

puter-chip brain was electronically linked in with TDH. In the event of a dangerous reading, an immediate alert was sent.

"Take it to the lab," Neshi ordered. "Give me a report in the morning."

"As you say," Cortuk replied.

As the lab tech was turning to leave, he kicked one of the rocks in the pile. This caused a minor avalanche, and the others tumbled away, revealing a large hole in the ground.

Neshi poked his head in first. The tunnel he saw leading south straightened out in a bit and then seemed to go east.

Cortuk volunteered to join Neshi. "It's been a dull week," he said, smiling.

The eastbound tunnel seemed to go on for some distance.

"Look!" Cortuk exclaimed.

Even dissipating as it was, the tube shed enough light to let them see ahead for hundreds of yards.

"Now we know what its use was," Neshi observed.

"The hunchback's escape route?"

"A very strong possibility, wouldn't you say?"

They walked some distance along the tunnel, noticing a scrap of food here, a garment there, a pair of foot coverings, and other items.

"I have a curious feeling, Tech Detective Neshi," Cortuk said.

"About what?"

"Some of the victims were never found. There was evidence of a struggle, but no bodies."

"I know."

"What if we stumble upon—"

His words were prophetic. Less than a minute later, an

oppressive odor assailed their nostrils. Cortuk gagged on it. "Like rotting—"

They turned a corner and saw where the unfound victims had been kept by the hunchback.

"I can't stay here," Cortuk said, his voice trembling badly. "I—" and then he became very ill.

Neshi was nearly overwhelmed by the sight of bodies that in some cases had been there, he guessed, for several weeks. Bits and pieces were scattered randomly; small furry creatures fed on several of them.

"I think we will need help," Cortuk said after getting himself together.

A split second after he spoke, an object came flying out of the darkness, landing in the middle of his back. A wide-bladed knife! He reached back and touched it, a stunned expression on his face. "Neshi, I've been—" he started to say before he collapsed to the ground.

Neshi bent over the lab tech.

"I always wanted to see a little action," Cortuk said. "You know, staying in a lab all the time can kill you."

He was dead seconds later.

As Neshi was standing up, he sensed something running at him from his blind side. Before he could defend himself, another body hit his own, and he was flung against the hard rock wall of the tunnel. His eyesight dimmed briefly, and he vaguely saw a figure dashing past him. When his vision cleared, it was gone, but he knew the direction in which it was headed.

He took out his beam-pistol,[3] holding it in his right

---

[3] Shaped like an elongated egg, it had a button on top and one end was flattened; when fired, by thumb action on the button, a laser beam emanated from the flat portion, the criminal dead before hitting the ground if hit in the heart or the temple.

hand. The tube's illumination was nearly gone. Then he noticed something sticking out of a side pocket in Cortuk's outer garment. A porta-glow![4]

It wasn't made for long distances, but a red flasher on the side would warn him when power was beginning to run low.

The farther Neshi walked along the tunnel, the more alarmed he became. What he saw was not merely evidence of madness but something beyond that, something he couldn't quite explain. Every so often he would stumble on arm bones and leg bones picked clean. He also saw intact skeletons dumped in one corner or another, plus half a dozen skulls without the rest of the bodies. There was always the odor of decay in the air.

Of all the violence in the past, of all the degeneracy, nothing compared with this.

He entered a small cavern littered with photographs, and what they showed brought a new wave of revulsion. Glass tanks filled with arms and legs and eyes. Tiny infants in sealed jars.

One of the photographs showed a pile of shattered glass. In its midst was something small but badly deformed, so grotesquely that he crumpled up that photograph and threw it to one side.

He had become so engrossed in the photos that, despite years of Tech Detective training, he was unaware of movement in the corridor opposite the one from which he had just come. Something hard hit the back of his head, and he stumbled and fell. Blood dribbled from his nose. He fought to hold onto consciousness.

---

[4] Essentially a nuclear-powered flashlight but with a striking range of penetration. The only problem was that its energy lasted for less than two hours before it had to be recharged.

As Neshi looked up, he saw, bending over him and holding a large rock, the object of his investigation: the hunchback.

His hooded face was witchlike, not at all male in appearance, and Neshi momentarily puzzled over that. The skin was a sick gray, tinged with mottled green, as though gangrenous. Several teeth were missing; others were dark with decay. One eye appeared to be clouded over with thin, pale, white tissue.

Neshi rolled over and the rock hit the ground less than an inch away.

"Who are you?" he screamed. "Why are you doing this?"

The hunchback laughed insanely, his twisted body covered by a cloak.

Neshi scrambled to his feet. As he was reaching for his beam-pistol, which he had reholstered while he was looking at the photos, the hunchback charged him again, with such speed that he wasn't prepared. He fell against the hard wall, the edge of a section of rock jamming sharply into his back. He let out a cry, tears of pain rolling down his cheeks.

The hunchback stepped back for a few seconds, looking at him curiously. Neshi pulled out the beam-pistol and started to depress the firing button.

Nothing!

Again.

Still nothing.

The pistol had jammed on him.

The hunchback walked slowly forward, reaching out one gnarled hand toward him. He was now inches away.

Neshi had an auxiliary weapon, an old-fashioned steel-bladed knife, like the one used to kill Cortuk. As he was reaching for it, the creature's left hand touched the tears on his cheek with surprising gentleness.

That was all the time an experienced Tech Detective needed. A strange expression of recognition showed on the hunchback's face. As he opened his mouth to speak, Neshi jabbed the knife into his stomach.

The grotesque yet pathetic creature fell forward against him. For an instant, he seemed to gather one last bit of strength, reached out, drew Neshi to him, and kissed the Tech Detective with an oddly familiar passion, the odor of his breath causing Neshi to gag. As his gaze met Neshi's, he spoke a single word, barely above a pain-streaked whisper: "Baba!" And then the hunchback crumpled to the ground at Neshi's feet.

Neshi stood there, shaking, still holding the knife, the front of his uniform blood-soaked. Then he dropped the weapon and bent over the body of the creature, pulling off the hood.

Not a male at all. A female, long hair tied together by crude string, very thin-faced, gaunt, the look of long illness written in lines on the forehead and dark circles under the eyes.

"You called me Baba," he said, his mind whirling. "How did you know that name?"

Her eyes widened as she pointed to the scar across the top of her temple.

"I—I don't understand," he told her. "Please, I—"

"Eta—" she said just before life flowed from her body.

He stood dizzily, the tunnel starting to wobble in his vision. He turned and ran back the way he had come, past Cortuk's still body, and outside, other Tech Detectives just then entering the alley.

"Neshi!" one of them exclaimed.

His whole being was on the edge of collapse. *Eta!* It could not be!

"Neshi, what went on back there?" another asked.

He couldn't speak at first, then he managed to mumble something like, "I don't want to talk about it."

He couldn't let them see him reacting as he was. No matter what the circumstances, no Tech Detective ever cracked under the strain. All applicants were given extensive psychiatric tests, with more attention paid to their emotional and psychological stamina than to their physical prowess and endurance. One of the tests involved putting each hopeful through a re-creation of what amounted to his worst nightmare. For some, it was falling from a tall building; for others, being buried alive; for a few, it was being forced to stand in a pit of poisonous crawling creatures. Everything was make-believe, of course, but done so realistically that the would-be Tech Detective came to believe that it was very real—and his reaction was given significant weight in the final decision to accept or reject him.

"Can we take you back to your quarters?" the other asked.

He could feel physical strength returning, though his mind was still devastated. "I'll walk," he said. "The night air will help."

"But a report, Neshi. You know we'll need a report."

"Tomorrow," he said. "I'll do it tomorrow."

The two other Tech Detectives exchanged glances but decided not to push the matter further.

Neshi thanked them and started walking out of the alley.

His housing unit was not a significant distance from The Dome. Once he left the less modern, wider thoroughfares of Old Town, the streets became narrow, with tall metallic-and-glass buildings and shorter commercial places on either side. At that time of night, mists rode in on breezes that came from the north, across the flat moors that comprised 70 percent or more of the surface of the planet—bleak stretches of barrenness with only bizarre forms of life capable of surviving in the dryness and the heat.

Neshi had had to pursue a criminal across the moors some time ago. He almost died before he cornered the felon. His orders had been for a live capture, but one of the creatures living in the outlands, a round ball-like thing with prickly projections covering it entirely, was disturbed and lodged itself in the back of the criminal's neck, driving several of those hollowed projections up into his brain. Death would have been slow and extremely painful as the creature drained its victim's bodily fluids directly into its own mass, which began to puff up. Out of a sense of mercy, Neshi lasered both of them, making especially sure that the felon did not linger. Other Tech Detectives might have perversely enjoyed the sight, but Neshi was different.

Indeed, it seemed that he was different from as far back as he could remember. He never enjoyed inflicting pain or watching its onslaught. So many in his profession deliberately lasered criminals in different parts of their body so death would come slowly. When there had to be a kill, Neshi did it with efficiency, believing in mercy.

He was becoming more and more resistant to the carnage that grew out of an increasingly violent society. Perhaps it was a by-product of that incessant nightmare and whatever subliminal meaning it held.

"Etarina," he whispered her name.

How could it be that he heard her nickname for him coming from the lips of a hideous hunchback? How could it be?

Dizziness returned. He barely made it to his apartment. Once inside, he sank down on the sofa in his living room and closed his eyes. A headache was pounding at him.

Sleep came quickly, with a different sort of nightmare accompanying it, images from reality that were every bit as horrible. . . .

6

There was no respite. Even if anyone had known what he had encountered, Neshi doubted there would be much official sympathy. The triumph of tracking down the hunchback murderer swept everything else away.

And so he was expected to become immersed in the fanfare that started early the next morning. A call from TDH indicated that he was to be at the mayor's media room for a news conference in one hour, where he would be required to sound noble and courageous for the media.

He mumbled agreement, hung up the telecall receiver, and remained sitting on the couch. It was not his normal place for sleeptime, yet he had been too traumatized the night before to do anything but collapse onto it, simply because it was the nearest piece of furniture.

Eta—

He wanted to believe that it was just a coincidence. He

59

could have been successful in that exercise—after all, there were other names beginning with those letters—if not for the second word uttered by the hunchback: *Baba!*

Nobody but Etarina knew that. It was a highly personal testament of affection, expressed verbally, between the two of them. But the loathsome being he had come face-to-face with, whose twisted hands had wrenched life from at least twenty citizens, couldn't have been further from the reality embodied by his beloved Etarina: physical beauty, emotional sensitivity, a personality exuding warmth and kindness.

Neshi shuddered at the thought of all those bodies ravaged by a single individual. As mandated by law, their limbs had been grafted to living bodies that needed them, their hearts in other chests, their brains—

Her eyes had widened as she pointed to the scar across the top of her temple.

He was standing as that thought coursed through his mind.

. . . across the top of her temple.

The impact of it nearly knocked him off his feet again, the room wavering. He stumbled forward, grabbing the back of a chair for stability.

"Fifty minutes! Fifty minutes!"

The strident sound of his schedule-mate broke the silence that had settled like a shroud. An automated computer chip, a schedule-mate was installed in the living quarters of each Tech Detective for the purpose of keeping him on schedule. The press conference was due to start in fifty minutes.

How can I make it?

Something Etarina had said during their brief honeymoon came back to him. Perhaps it was a premonition on her part. "I hope we are together for a very long time, my love. But unless we die together, one of us will someday face life alone, and it will be awful. But, remember, dear Neshi—remember what we did have. It will not be the same as our lips actually touching, as our arms around each other, as our hearts beating in rhythm together. But if not in the flesh, then in the mind; if not in life, then in memory."

She had been standing on the balcony of their apartment, looking out beyond the city to the patch of desolate moors visible between the tall buildings. The mist rising from them had seemed thicker than usual, and the air was quite chill. She didn't remain there long; when she turned to go inside, he saw that she had been crying.

He had asked her what was wrong.

"Wrong, dear one? No, no, everything is so right. These are not tears of grief. I have never been happier in all my life."

That was only three years before.

He had come very close to abandoning everything, to telling the mayor and his superiors at TDH that he was quitting, and then, somehow, disappearing, away from the media, away from the scum he had been hunting for so long, from everybody else in that city and on that world—and perhaps, perhaps willing himself to death in order to avoid facing any more of a life lived without his beloved.

But if not in the flesh, then in the mind; if not in life, then in memory.

Should he die early, retreating into what Thought and Spirit called the Currents of the Cosmos, life shut off forever, then Etarina would be absolutely dead as a separate and identifiable personality, his memories of her ceasing with his last heartbeat as he supposedly joined some sort of eternal stream. That might well happen ultimately, of course, but Etarina deserved to live *as* Etarina in the synapses of his brain as long as he could manage it.

After facing the reporters and the photographers as ingenuously as possible, Neshi was taken to a special luncheon in his honor and given a seat next to Mayor Gursack.

"You could be in for a promotion," Gursack whispered.

"Is that the case, sir?" he said in a deliberate monotone.

"It is, Neshi, it is. You are being considered as International Director after Hukien retires shortly."

Despite the emotional upheaval of the past twenty-four-hour period, that news cut through to Neshi's core of sensibilities. International Director of the Tech Detectives Division! That meant being in charge of the entire planet.

His face flushed with surprise. "I hardly deserve that for one case," he feebly protested.

"Skip the modesty," Gursack snorted. "You have an exemplary record, the best by far that TDH has ever seen, I am told. Who else is there? That wimp Tushur? TDH would go downhill very rapidly if he were at the helm."

The mayor had a point. If Tushur were the other choice, well, Neshi knew that the mayor's gloomy words could prove to be prophetic.

"I am glad to serve when and as called, sir."

"Fine, fine," Gursack said, winking at him. "I'll make sure an announcement is issued from TDH less than twenty-four hours after Hukien leaves the job. And we all thank you, Neshi. These are times that stress the need for someone of your caliber to guard the safety of us all."

After the luncheon had ended, Neshi went back to the privacy of his office and shut the door behind him.

"If only you could be here to share this," he said out loud as he sat down at his desk.

He looked out the window at the crowds on the street

below, males and females returning to work after their own breaks. He couldn't see any of their faces.

A sudden thought nibbled at the edges of the equilibrium that was slowly reestablishing itself: *Who out there was walking around with Etarina's heart?* Who would one day look at him, unknowingly, with her eyes? Who would have her hands and shake his own?

He turned away from the window.

Her lungs were still breathing as before. Her stomach—

He sat down, looking blankly at the papers piled on his desk.

And her brain. It would go into another body if it had not been damaged. And perhaps yet someone else would leave notes, hoping that he would find them. And if that individual died before he did, poor, tragic Etarina's mind, the center of her being, would be passed along, perhaps again and again, until one day it simply wore out and had to be discarded.

The buzzing of his telecall unit shook him out of his reverie.

"Neshi, congratulations!"

It was Ferene. "Forgive me for not attending the luncheon. I've had a bit of a bug."

"Sorry to hear that," Neshi replied as nonchalantly as he could manage.

"Have you played that film strip as yet?"

"No, I haven't."

"But then you've had your hands full, of course. Would you be able to get to it tonight, as a special favor?"

"Count on it, Ferene."

"Talk to you later. And thanks."

Curiosity crowded out the morbidity that had temporarily seized Neshi.

7

He returned to his apartment after spending the rest of the day at TDH. Once inside, he quickly sat down at his desk and slipped the plastic strip into his compuview machine.

It was a fragment of a classified report. If someone else had seen it before Ferene, they would surely have destroyed it, and the careless individual responsible would have been severely reprimanded.

"As the attacks intensify, the Departure Date can be adjusted according to the circumstances," he read.

Neshi repeated three words to himself: *the Departure Date.*

The fragment continued: "It should be during sleep-time, of course; it is then that we can immobilize, or if necessary—"

He could not believe the next few words, but they were there, on the viewer like an obscene finger in his face.

" . . . terminate the entire populace."

He pushed himself back from the viewer, perspiration drenching him. Then he played back that last sequence.

"It should be during sleeptime, of course; it is then that we can immobilize, or if necessary, terminate the entire populace."

But how? Millions of citizens! How could they all be terminated at the same time?

Just then the communication center rang shrilly. Neshi stood, walked over to the far wall, and pressed the appropriate button.

It was Ferene. "Have you—"

"Yes," Neshi interrupted him. "Yes, I have. When should we meet?"

"Tomorrow at midnight."

"Where?"

"At the catacombs."

"The—"

"Please—trust me."

"I'll be there, Ferene."

Neshi disconnected and stood there shivering.

Much later that night, after he could fight tiredness no longer, he undressed and approached the cylinder in his sleep room, realizing he hadn't been in it for two nights. It was six and one-half feet long, dull gray in color. The top third opened up at his command and he climbed inside, the warmth of the fluids reassuring him as his body sank down into them.

"Close," he said out loud.

The lid slowly came down over him as he remembered

the words from the report fragment: "It should be during sleeptime, of course." They played back in his mind again and again, like a broken audio disc, repeating over and over. His mind raced over the possibilities. What more defenseless period? As most of the populace was surrounded by—

Of course!

By then it was too late for Neshi. The seductive pull of the fluids, warm, reassuring; the isolation; the gentle vibration motion . . . he was beyond waking, at that moment, already sent into what the nighttime held for him.

The instrument panel had been crafted with noteworthy attention to detail. The pre-Tekkies were amazed.

"It's so complete you wonder why they've never put it in the real thing," the one next to Neshi remarked.

"I can hardly wait to get down and work with those controls," Neshi said, "even if they are phony."

"But why the waste of time and money on just a toy?"

"Who can say?" Neshi answered with a shrug of his shoulders.

There were no strange dreams that night, only that memory of an incident from his training days and after that, just a kind of discomforting oblivion, not at all like the restful sleeptime intended. With the approach of daylight, as Neshi climbed out of the cylinder, he felt momentarily surprised that he was alive.

He decided to check into Tech Detective Headquarters earlier than usual. Rather than go on a hunt that day, he wanted to spend some time in the Hall of Knowledge

Division before it became so busy that even he would have to stand in line.

The Hall of Knowledge was a rather small room with a rounded ceiling, certainly not as grand as its name implied. There were two levels. On each level were small, semicircular booths, and in each booth was a compuview machine linked to the central depository of all the knowledge that had ever been recorded since the beginnings of civilization on that planet.

Tech Detectives could gain access to virtually everything in that depository; it was a mark of the privilege Neshi and others like him enjoyed. The average citizen's access was much more limited.

Neshi coded in his number on the keypad in front of him, then typed in the words *sleeptime cylinders*.

"Sleeptime cylinders were invented six decades ago by individuals from the Chemists Guild and the Electro-Powerites."

Neshi found that quite amazing. Only sixty years! He would have thought they were much less recent than that, going back a number of centuries, in fact.

He read on from the screen in front of him: "Specifically at the request of the Natasians. . . ."

What? The smallest group of politicians in the entire government. How could they bring about anything as comprehensive as this?

The rest of the information seemed to be almost entirely technical: the design of the cylinders, the composition of the fluids.

The fluids, he said to himself. *What in fact are they made up of?*

The ingredients were listed in their entirety. Nothing sinister there.

Next he went on to the electrowiring makeup of the cylinders. Everything once again seemed—

Wait! he told himself.

All electro-energy came from the government's central power plants. Could that be a clue? He momentarily chuckled at himself, realizing that he was slipping into the syndrome of seeing something sinister in every detail, no matter how inconsequential.

Absurd, he thought finally. *This is absurd. Why am I believing all this nonsense?*

He was about to leave the booth, disgruntled, when he decided, as an afterthought, to look up the word *Jerusalem.*

"No admittance. Restricted data. No admittance."

Neshi scratched his neck in puzzlement. He tried again. Still the same response. Restricted even for a Tech Detective of his status! Having patience for only one more try, he typed out: *Natasians.*

The usual dry facts were presented: the date of their origin as a political faction, the number of members, and so on—plus one other bit of information: "Natasians all have come from one of two guilds: the Chemists and the Electro-Powerites."

The same guilds that pushed for the use of the sleeptime cylinders six decades ago! Neshi sat back in the comfortably cushioned chair in the booth.

The Chemists had invented the fluids that were comprised of such innocent-sounding ingredients. The Electro-Powerites were responsible for maintaining the power running the whole society. Together they pushed through legislation requiring citizens to use the cylinders!

Perfectly ordinary information. And yet when combined together!

Still nothing.

Those factors bespoke nothing overtly sinister, as far as Neshi could ascertain. The only sinister elements were in the plastic fragment Ferene had given him, and in Ferene's very manner. What did it all mean? Hopefully his friend would be able to help him.

8

The catacombs were left over from the initial settlement of the planet eons ago, reminders of the very primitive beginnings of a civilization that had grown to surpassing technological advancement in more recent times. They were both historical treasures and embarrassments, since the government's mentality was not "Look how far we have come since then" but "Look how backward we once were!"

Neshi needed an airmobile to travel the distance to the closest section of catacombs. As a Tech Detective, all he had to do was put in a call to headquarters and one would be sent to him within five minutes. Only a few citizens could afford private airmobiles; the rest had to depend on so-called public transportation.

The vehicle was waiting for him by the time he left the elevator. It had been sent by autopilot. As soon as he climbed inside, he was able to override that mechanism and take direct control himself. The airmobile was oblong in shape, suitable for the driver and one passenger. It could attain a top speed of 195 miles per hour, its aerodynamic design virtually flawless.

Neshi started it by voice control; the steering was done by hand. Additionally, he could raise or lower the top by voice. He chose to have the top down.

One problem his world did not have was air pollution. The atmosphere was well-nigh self-purgative of whatever contaminants tried to linger. Moreover, it had a decidedly healing effect on the body of each citizen, so he enjoyed savoring it as the airmobile glided quietly through the streets. The vehicle, which floated a foot or so off the ground, was powered by air, which meant it was incapable of pollution and its engine outlasted anything else his people had ever invented.

Few citizens walked the streets at night anymore. Whispers about the roving gangs had sent waves of caution through the populace. But there was actually more to it than that. Inside their domiciles, his people had just about everything they could want in terms of entertainment. They ventured out to buy clothes, food, and so on, and to go to the weekly games at The Dome, but not for much more.

Which was why Neshi was so surprised to see a greater number than usual outside that night—couples walking leisurely, some with children, others taking care of the needs of their pets, a few strolling by themselves.

He pulled over to the curb and summoned one young couple.

"Can we help you, Tech Detective?" they asked in unison, seeing his uniform.

"Please, yes. There is much activity tonight. Is there something special going on?"

"No, sir," the male answered. "Until The Dome is repaired, we thought we would spend some spare time just enjoying the walk. The air, you know."

Neshi nodded, thanked the two of them, and drove off.

"Just enjoying the walk."

Somehow those words were more encouraging than he could have imagined. Take away The Dome and, contrary to government research, you did not have immediate chaos and crime in the streets.

Neshi smiled, the air that night seeming sweeter than ever.

The catacombs.

He approached them at reduced speed, circling the entrances once, twice, a third time, and then stopping the airmobile a few hundred feet away.

The entrances were set in the sides of a series of hills, natural caves that led deep within the earth.

Neshi had his beam-pistol set to active status, just in case.

Several minutes passed. Ferene was late. More time went by. Neshi was becoming annoyed. Had Ferene concocted some bizarre practical joke?

More than twenty minutes after he was supposed to be there, Ferene's airmobile pulled up next to Neshi's.

"Really glad you showed up," Ferene said, coming at a run.

They shook hands.

"What is going on, my friend?" Neshi asked, his annoyance quickly forgotten.

"I can fill you in on some of the details, but others will do the rest."

"What others?"

"Patience, Neshi. Now is the time to show a little of that patience the government supposedly trained into you. First, though, we must talk about someone once very close to you."

"You mean Etarina, don't you?"

"I do."

"She was the one behind—"

"The hunchback murders. I know."

"How could you, Ferene?"

Ferene indicated two flat rocks a few feet away. "Sit down, my friend. Please."

Neshi consented, and Ferene joined him.

"Come right out with it," Neshi insisted.

"We stumbled upon Etarina one night quite by accident."

"We?"

"Yes, yours truly and some others. We have dubbed ourselves the Jerusalemites. You see, many of us have dreamed as you have. Hence, our name."

"You!"

"I am one of them, Neshi. I must tell you that. There can be no more deception between us. You can take me into custody, if you must."

"Don't be foolish, Ferene. I'm just—"

"Surprised? I had no doubt that you would be. Imagine, though, my amazement when we found Etarina. That, I assure you, was a shocker worthy of the name. She came in from the moors and ended up near the catacombs."

"The moors? But how could she have survived?"

"There is no way of knowing. That was many months

74

ago, Neshi. Several of my fellows spotted her and took her in. She was babbling at first, but eventually she calmed down. Initially there was no way of telling who or what she was."

"But Etarina was so ravishing. This pathetic—"

"If you were about to say *creature*, you would be closer to the truth than you could ever suppose. You see, Neshi, what we have been told down through the years is only partially true. Bodily organs are used to replace damaged ones in citizens who have had accidents, have suffered from brain tumors or disease, or whatever."

"What have we not been told?"

"Experiments. Most of the organs are being used in experiments."

"For what purpose, Ferene?"

"The creation of new life in a laboratory."

"By whom?"

"The Natasians."

"But why? Artificial insemination has been around for a long time."

"Not that sort of life, Neshi. They seem to be convinced that we are not as advanced as we might think. Having more of the same is of no interest to the Natasians. What they are pursuing is some sort of super race, a race with some ingredient that we supposedly are missing. But they haven't been able to figure out just what that is."

. . . *littered with photographs, and what they showed brought a new wave of revulsion.*

Glass tanks filled with arms and legs and eyes.

Tiny infants in sealed jars.

One of the photographs showed a pile of shattered glass. In its midst was something small but badly deformed, so gro-

tesquely that he crumpled up that photograph and threw it to one side.

"Ferene, I have some photos," Neshi offered.

"Tell me about them."

After Neshi described what he saw in the tunnel, Ferene exhaled loudly. "But something has invariably gone wrong. They've not been able to get it right after many years of trying. What has always resulted is—"

"A hunchback?"

"Or a baby with no limbs. Or some creature with two heads." Ferene cleared his throat, then continued. "What I suspect they did in Etarina's case was place her brain in a body that they had managed to grow."

"And then what happened?"

"The transplantation went awry, as it has always done in such instances. It's almost as though a hidden force has stood in the way, not wanting the natural and normal to be violated. In any event, she started to change, but slowly. She became all twisted, bones out of shape, pain in every movement. Her mind went eventually, Neshi. It was horrible to see all this happening in front of our eyes, especially since, at the start, though in a different body, enough of the Etarina you knew had survived, and she was endearing."

"Was she able to tell you all this?" Neshi interrupted.

"Hardly. She knew only scraps of the truth. We have been able to gather more information from inside sources as well as contacts with other creations that have managed to escape."

"Was Etarina aware of—"

"I don't think it is necessary to—"

"To tell me everything? I need to know, Ferene. I beg you, my friend, tell me all of it."

76

"Etarina still carried her memories of you. She was completely aware of what was going on. As she was escaping, she saw herself in a mirror. Neshi, I can't go on with this."

Neshi had gotten to his feet and was pacing. "Was she able to talk about our love?"

"Yes. Those were the moments she was the most coherent."

Ferene stood as well. "Etarina was tormented by those memories. She relived them over and over, Neshi, and yet she comprehended, in the midst of her growing madness— I suspect that is what drove her over the edge—the fact that she could never hold you in her arms again."

"But she left notes."

"I know that, Neshi."

"You do?"

"Here is one of them. It was left after she managed to elude us as cleverly as she did the Natasians."

Neshi's hand trembled as he took the scrap of paper. The writing was quite scrawly but not obscured by water and dirt: "Baba, my love for you lives, dear one. It does."

"Etarina was caught between a desire to keep you in the dark and a desperate compulsion to tell you before it was too late."

"Tell me what?"

"About what is going on. So you could do something about it, stop it, save others from the kind of nightmare she was enduring. And so you could stop her."

"From murdering any more of the innocent? Those murders were a result of the madness that was overwhelming her!"

"That is so, Neshi. But there was something else. She had convinced herself that you were the key. She wanted you to do something to end the horror for herself, and not incidentally for others going through a similar ordeal. Brains are being passed to another body and then another, and all the while those involved are *aware* of it. Think of that, Neshi. Think of actually being aware of what was going on each time."

"But I didn't. Now they've taken her again and put her—" He realized that he was on the verge of becoming hysterical. With an exercise of sheer willpower, Neshi brought his emotions under control.

"Do you want to go back?" Ferene asked sympathetically.

Neshi shook his head.

"You can, you know. We could come back here tomorrow night."

"You are a Jerusalemite," Neshi was able to say. "You and the others want to change this society. Perhaps I can help."

Ferene reached out and hugged Neshi, then they turned toward the catacombs, approaching the nearest of the cave entrances.

"Me first," Ferene said. "They need to see me before they do you."

The odor in the catacombs was that of thousands of years of death. Surrounding Neshi and Ferene on both sides were the remains of the original settlers of the planet, each placed in an excavated portion of the hard rock walls of the tunnel that headed gradually deeper.

Some of the skeletal figures, partially wrapped in a gauzelike material that had rotted away with the passage of time, were full-size; some were quite small, signifying youth. A number of the excavations were larger and contained three, even four figures, presumably entire families that had indicated a desire to be buried together.

"It was pretty terrible in those days," Ferene spoke softly. "They came from a place radically different from this planet. Before they entered the caves, many died aboveground, unaccustomed to the heat of a sun which was much more intense then. The air tended to be healing, but the sun was too powerful. Today it is our benefactor, its radiance milder—but then it was a merciless destroyer."

And so refuge was sought in the catacombs. They had to eat many of the native species, often loathsome creatures of darkness, in order to stay alive, life forms it was almost impossible to look at without fear or disgust, and yet these had to be cooked and swallowed, sometimes even eaten raw.

Neshi shivered as he remembered that frequently the original settlers had resorted to cannibalism in order to stay alive.

"Why go you after me? Why reach out with your skeletal arms and your unholy tongues, seeking—"

How much of his nightmare was based on half-forgotten bits of knowledge about the original settlers?

On and on the tunnel went. Neshi was becoming tired and more than a little claustrophobic. He had to fight the compulsion to flee the bodies on both sides, the distinctive odor of death, the darkness only partially dispelled by the flashtube Ferene brought along, all this reinforcing the feeling of one huge tomb that, if they did not leave, would somehow claim them both.

"Ferene, I think—" he started to say, when suddenly he saw the first indistinct figure moving in the darkness ahead.

"I'll talk first," Ferene whispered.

Neshi offered no protest.

9

The first figure, now lit by the beam of Ferene's flash-tube as well as its own source of illumination, a hopelessly antiquated eternaflame cylinder hanging from his right hand, seemed not much different from anyone else of Neshi's race, just dirtier, with clothes that were little more than rags.

"Ah, he came!" the figure exclaimed, obviously appreciative.

"Yes, Nuath, but after he learned of the terrible tragedy involving his mate, Etarina," Ferene said. "We need to be as considerate as we can, my friend."

Within a couple of minutes, there were others like him, quite unkempt and yet uncommonly friendly. After all, he was one of the more celebrated Tech Detectives whose duties included tracking down roving bands of rebels.

Nuath sensed his puzzlement. "We accept you because we know you."

"Know me? How could you?"

"From reports."

"The media?"

"Yes. And otherwise."

The way he said "otherwise" seemed more than a little cryptic, but Neshi let it pass.

"Come, let me introduce you to part of our Jerusalemite council," Nuath commented, proceeding to point out the others: Yuane, Girad, Zeemir, and Sucer.

Neshi and Ferene followed them down a separate corridor to a huge cavern several levels tall. On each level sat scores of Jerusalemites, each with an eternaflame cylinder stuck into the rock in front of him.

Nuath got to the point quickly. "We need your help," he said.

"Aren't I a bit unlikely a choice for that?"

"You are the perfect choice, Tech Detective Neshi."

"I don't know if I can agree with you," he said, caution guiding him. "How can you be so sure that I am the least bit interested in overthrowing an elected government?"

At that, a general roar of laughter arose throughout the cavern, echoes mixing eerily.

"We understand you were not a supporter of The Dome games even before The Dome ended up in ashes."

"That is correct. But my lack of support for one policy is hardly grounds for presupposing that I want to have a new government installed."

"But that one policy matter is symptomatic of something else, is it not?"

Neshi was feeling a growing sense of discomfort. This individual, who appeared to be no more than a barbarian, spoke as though well educated, and he was touching upon some truths that Neshi had been only partially successful in ignoring.

"Tech Detective Neshi," Nuath persisted, "do you know why the Jerusalemites came into being?"

"My fellows and I were taught that it was because of an unwillingness to abide by established law."

There was a sound throughout the chamber again, but it was not laughter this time, rather, a roar of protest.

"That is only a partial statement of truth."

"You are either willing to be governed by the law or you are not. What is partial about that?"

"What it creates is an image of unfettered law*lessness*. All of us here, and others I will show you, and those no longer with us but taken by death, came very close to worshiping the law until we realized what it was designed to achieve."

"Order and social longevity."

More laughter again.

"Dictatorship of the most infamous sort."

Nuath cleared his throat, then continued. "Few have noticed the creeping nature of this cancer. Few have dared to come to grips with the realities confronting them day after day after day."

"And what has made you all so enlightened?"

"We all have lost family and friends to the Natasians." Nuath's voice was losing its pedantic tone, becoming angry.

"Lost? But how?"

What Nuath said next caused Neshi's body to be literally soaked in perspiration. "You see, they went to sleep and never again awoke!"

Neshi turned away, his temples pounding.

He felt a hand on his shoulder: Ferene.

"I've known about this for some time, Neshi. Yet I could not approach you until I was certain that you might be interested and, even more importantly, that you wouldn't betray us once you were told."

"Are you so sure about that, Ferene?"

"I would stake my life on it."

"There was a time when you would have been unwise to do that."

"No longer?"

"No longer."

Neshi stayed with them for several more hours, until just before daybreak.

He had been prepared at the outset to leave the Jerusalemites without accepting their offer. In fact, he was prepared, after listening politely, to reject it altogether, and, despite the loss of Etarina, go back to the way of life he had known for many years, and with which he had been comfortable, to a greater or lesser degree—that is, until he learned the reason for the sleeptime termination of countless numbers of their family members and friends.

"We have had strange dreams," Nuath told him, "dreams dealing with the Natasians, dreams that spur us on to rebellion."

"Nighttime fantasies caused all of this?" Neshi said incredulously. "Nothing more substantial than that?"

"We've counted them as warnings that the Natasians are far more evil than any of us would ever dare to imagine, even now!"

"Warnings must come from somewhere, from someone," Neshi pointed out, a note of sarcasm creeping into his voice. "Have you figured that part of it out as yet?"

Without answering that question, Nuath posed another: "Have you ever had a dream so compelling, so vivid that you were convinced it was more than idle fantasy?"

Neshi hesitated, knowing how close to home that question was.

"Your silence speaks volumes," Nuath said. "It is not just the dreams that make us strike out against the Natasians but a growing ability to interpret their content."

"And what do these moments of interpretation lead you to believe?" Neshi inquired.

"That the Natasians are not merely a relatively recent group of upstarts but have been with us for a very long time."

"How long?" Neshi prodded.

"Perhaps since the beginning of life here."

"Anything else?"

"That they are not confined just to our one world in a universe of countless millions of worlds."

"There are Natasians elsewhere, in other galaxies?" Ferene interceded.

"Please, my friend, we do not perceive *everything*. I ask you not to hold us accountable for the unknown. What I *can* say is that the Natasians are alarmed by these dreams, alarmed even more by our mushrooming ability to analyze the details with greater and greater perception."

"You must be getting even closer to some enormous truth that the Natasians fear," Neshi suggested.

"Precisely," Ferene said. "Those who have died through nighttime terminations are largely the ones who have evidenced the sharpest intuition about the Natasians. Before they rebel, before they join us, they are murdered. But still, the Natasians cannot get to everyone who dreams in such a revealing manner. A few manage to escape before the trap is sprung."

"Every Jerusalemite has this sensitivity?" Neshi asked.

"No! Many do but not all."

Neshi cleared his throat, finally deciding to admit his own persistent visions in the night.

"Let me tell you about my dream," Neshi said, clearing his throat. "No, it is a nightmare."

And then the most extraordinary thing happened in that cavern deep below the surface.

"I stood at the gate to a city with a wall around it," shouted one of those present.

"It was thrice my height," said another. "As I approached—"

"I could detect the odors immediately—"

And so it went until only Ferene had not spoken.

He stood, asking with a gesture that Neshi do likewise.

Ferene's eyes locked in on Neshi's as he said, "The sounds, whispering yet insistent, forming words that would haunt me well into the day following."

He turned to the others, and they all spoke the final seven words in unison: "*Jerusalem, Jerusalem, how I weep for thee.*"

Then only Ferene's voice could be heard. "Neshi, Neshi, good friend, we suspect that the nightmare is not merely an idle vision, however terrifying, inherited from the past but something from the future—a prophecy!"

Neshi looked at the figures around and above him, half seen in the flickering light cast by their eternaflames, part of his own race but outcasts because of their special gift.

"But the enemy spear? Does that not mean that *you* are the enemy, coming to destroy, not rescue?"

"We thought that at first, and it greatly troubled us. We

did not want to be the catalysts in a self-fulfilling prophecy, coming to redeem and ending up as the enemy."

Ferene motioned for Yuane to step forward. "Enlighten Tech Detective Neshi about your vision," Ferene said to the other. "Show him that we are the victims but not the enemy, surely not the enemy."

Yuane sat down on the bare ground, closing his eyes. "I am in a vast dark place of nothingness and dread." As he spoke, sweat came out in very large beads on his forehead and then his cheeks. "I want to scream, but I cannot. Words will not come."

As Yuane continued, he described being confronted by awful beings with claws and tails and cloven feet. They took him to a mountain from which he could see a terrible battle taking place. "It is the Day of Armageddon, they tell me. A field of blood spreads out before me."

And then the scene changed, and he was in a place of flame, cries rending the air with agony. "A huge figure is in front of me. It turns—and the loathsomeness of what I see—" Yuane was shivering "—boils erupting with pus like geysers from one of the sea creatures."

Yuane's eyes opened suddenly. He stood, turning to the others, then looking at Ferene, Nuath, and finally, Neshi. Especially Neshi.

"This monster comes toward me and says—oh, it says what my mind cannot fathom. It reaches out to me as though to embrace me, and it—" Yuane's eyes widened "—it cackles with glee as it tells me I am his, because *he has ownership of our souls!*"

Yuane was very weak.

"He owns our souls, Neshi, because long ago we rejected the one and true—"

And with that Yuane gripped his forehead with both

hands and collapsed into an unconscious heap on the ground.

Neshi stood outside in front of the catacombs, his head thrown back, his eyes searching the skies. "Ferene, from whence came such a race as we?" he asked, almost absentmindedly.

"We may never know," his friend replied. "It could have been one of a dozen, a hundred, a thousand worlds."

"Sufficient unto this planet are the evils thereof," Neshi added perversely. He breathed in deeply. "Ferene, there is much more to learn, isn't there? Much that they haven't as yet told me, or even know."

"Indeed that is correct, Neshi. Let me send you back to your apartment with one further thought."

"Yes?"

"On that plastic fragment were the words *Departure Date*. Have you any idea how that piece fits into this puzzle?"

Neshi shook his head. "And you?"

"Nothing concrete. Only the vaguest of suspicions."

"Care to share them with me?"

"Not as yet. We must never give birth to anything that borders on the irrational through the midwife of words spoken ignorantly. What I am thinking falls into that category, unless I am correct."

"And if you are?"

"The future is more bleak than we thought, unless—" Ferene stopped himself.

"Unless I become some kind of savior. Isn't that what you are about to say?" Neshi prompted.

"Yes, but it would have been unfair pressure on my part. Your decision has to be a free one, its consequences irreversible. Nothing like that should be shoved down anyone's throat."

Neshi smiled appreciatively. "Thank you, Ferene, but I still don't see what visits upon me such a monumental task."

"Frankly I don't think we know. Your name came to us, I sometimes think, almost on the air. We simply *knew*."

"Just a hunch, then."

"No, a prophecy."

They parted for the time being. For Neshi, the ride back to his apartment was one of confused thoughts mixed with a sense of unsettledness about what the coming weeks would hold.

In the past, when he was on a particularly upsetting case, he would feel uneasy, but never with such intensity. And always, at the end of the day, he would be able to climb into the sleeptime cylinder and feel the tensions literally float away. But now, that cylinder and what it portended was part of the problem and no longer the solution.

10

Neshi had free rein within TDH. There was little in his activities that others wouldn't take for granted. The first stop he made was to see a male named Quintez.

"Hi," he said as he entered the latter's smallish lab.

"What do you want?" the tall and bone-thin Quintez growled as he bent over a laserscope, an instrument with enormous magnification capabilities.

"Friendly as ever!" Neshi exclaimed.

"I'm on a case."

"Who isn't?"

Quintez started chuckling.

"You're right about that," he said as he looked up. "Sorry about the mood."

"We all have them."

"You, the celebrated Tekkie?"

"One case doesn't solve all the problems."

"But what a case!"

They talked a bit longer, and then Neshi slipped in some questions he had had in mind from the beginning.

"The transplantation scheme. What can you tell me about it?"

"Probably nothing you don't already know."

"Try me."

"It's the way our government devised to maximize resources."

"Bureaucratic platitudes! Come on now, Quintez."

"I don't know where to start. What specific area of transplantation do you have in mind?"

"The failure rate."

"There are no failures."

"That's hard to swallow."

"Officially, that is."

"Try unofficially."

Quintez seemed to be somewhat uncomfortable at that point. "The failures are redistributed so that the record shows up as a perfect score, you might say."

"What kinds of failures have you heard about?"

"Rejection of organs, or heart attacks coming after acceptance of a transplanted organ. This was not a problem of the refusal of one body to take in an organ from another, but rather the strain on the transplanted organ itself."

"And the ones that don't work are simply recycled in the hope that the right combination is eventually found?"

"Correct. Unless the organ has been severely damaged."

"What if it is only moderately damaged?"

"Well, if it replaces one that has been rendered completely useless, the transplantation goes on anyway."

"So there is transplantation of defective organs from time to time?"

"Often," Quintez said in a whisper. "Expediency is what counts."

Neshi thanked him and was about to leave when Quintez motioned him into the freezer compartment of his lab and shut the door behind him.

"Isn't there a more subtle way of giving me a cold shoulder?" Neshi joked.

Quintez didn't laugh. "There's more, friend," he said. "Think of this. What happens in the name of expediency when a bureaucrat has liver trouble? A transplant is needed. But at that particular juncture of events, none are immediately available."

"So the bureaucrat dies."

"Don't bet on it."

"What are you saying?" Neshi felt a chill that had nothing to do with the temperature in the freezer locker.

"Healthy sources of organs are being sought constantly. And if the bureaucrat rates higher on the government's scale of personal worth than, say, a laborer or some other lowly individual?"

"You can't be serious!"

"Answer my questions with the first thought that comes to your mind, Neshi."

Neshi's gaze drifted about the locker. Body parts were kept there—arms and legs and livers and hearts, mostly damaged ones—for autopsy and other purposes.

"Are you suggesting that citizens are being murdered?"

"*Murder* is not the operative word, Neshi. *Execution* is preferred. Or—"

The thought seemed to speed from Quintez's brain to Neshi's in an instant. "The games!"

Quintez nodded. "The games were started as much for the goal of guaranteeing a fresh supply of organs as for their stated purpose of offering vicarious release for the violent tendencies of a frustrated populace."

The chillness was getting to them. They left the locker, and Quintez shut the door behind him. "I feel more secure in there," he said. "Anything more I can help you with, Tech Detective Neshi?"

Neshi thanked him again and left.

Another thought was nagging at him: *With the games temporarily ceasing as a result of the collapse of The Dome, how desperate would the transplantation situation become in the eyes of the bureaucrats? And what would be done to alleviate it?*

Neshi stopped at the Hall of Knowledge again. This time he dialed up some current statistics. It had been less than two weeks since The Dome disaster. What had happened to the crime rate since then? He had seen citizens walking the streets in apparent relief, seemingly no more prone to violence than before.

Robberies down! Rapes on the decrease as well! Crimes of passion plummeting by 50 percent!

He looked through the statistics again. Indeed! Since the games had stopped, the rate was less in all but one category: murder!

Murders had increased greatly. Those figures on the screen in front of him stood out as pure anachronism. Everything else had dropped except the most violent crime of all! With the games over for the moment, the bureaucrats had to look elsewhere for their body parts. Somehow the word *coincidence* didn't even enter his mind.

*   *   *

Later, in his office at TDH, Neshi called a counterpart of his at TDH in another city.

"Mirkus, hello!" he said as cheerfully as he could fake.

"Neshi, it's been ages," Mirkus said over the receiver.

"I'm trying to get a handle on something. Willing to help me?"

"Absolutely. Just ask."

"The games in your city. There's been no problem, has there?"

"None at all. Strong as ever. Are you feeling it where you are? What happened there at your Dome is the talk of the planet."

"That's part of my reason for calling, Mirkus. Tell me, what's the murder rate like where you are?"

"I'll look it up."

Several seconds passed.

"Latest info," Mirkus said, returning to the receiver, "shows a decline. Has it been increasing your way?"

"Straight up the chart."

"The games help after all, I guess."

"Seems that way. Thanks, friend."

"Anytime, Neshi. You're the best."

Neshi made other calls to additional contacts in other cities. His last call was the most interesting.

"Ormit," he said, "this is Neshi. Sorry for the long silence."

"Any Tekkie who tracks down the hunchback must have had his hands full. No problem. What's on your mind?"

Neshi asked about the games.

"Yeh, there's been a problem."

"What sort?"

"We had a minor earthquake here three weeks ago."

"I remember hearing something about it."

"Just strong enough to knock out the electricity in and around our Dome. It'll be back in action this week, though."

"Tell me about the murder rate during the same period."

"I don't even have to look it up, Neshi. I've been busy enough going after the criminals."

"A lot greater?"

"Saying 'a lot' is understating it, believe me. Interesting difference, though."

"How so?"

"They've been primarily mutilation cases."

A bell rang loudly in Neshi's brain. "Are you sure?"

"Sure as my name, rank, and serial number."

Neshi thanked him and slowly hung up the receiver. After he stopped trembling, he phoned Quintez.

A strange voice answered.

"Quintez, please," he asked.

"Quintez is no longer in this department."

"What? Are you certain?"

"Indeed. I am his replacement. He has been arrested. My name is—"

Neshi didn't wait.

He left earlier than usual that day, anxious to get back to his apartment, to sit alone and think. It was still daylight, so he walked instead of taking a TDH vehicle.

Quintez arrested! So suddenly. Perhaps he had been under suspicion for some time.

He thought back to what Ormit had told him about the incidence of mutilation cases. He had been so stunned that he neglected to ask about what sort of mutilations had occurred. The whole grisly cavalcade was overwhelming. He almost hated to call Ormit at home, hated to find out more details. But he did so anyway.

Every Tech Detective had a listing of information about every other one on the entire planet, including their home communication numbers. He found Ormit's quickly. At first there was no response. As he was about to hang up, Ormit finally answered. "Had some bad food," he explained. "Been running to the bathroom every few minutes. Can't talk long."

"Those mutilation murders—" Neshi started to say.

"I'm so sick, Neshi. Can't we—"

"It's crucial, Ormit."

"Knowing you, I guess I can accept that totally. Don't misunderstand if I have to interrupt every so often."

"Okay. Here's what I'm hoping you can tell me: In how many of the cases that you remember were any organs missing?"

"That's an easy one."

"It is? Why?"

"Because all the cases were alike in that regard."

"Alike?"

"Yes. Organs were missing in each and every instance."

"The same ones?"

"No. With some, it was a heart, with others, a liver. With a couple, the eyes."

Neshi gulped.

"Neshi, are we still connected?"

"Yes."

"You sound worse than I feel! What's wrong?"

"I'm not sure."

Ormit groaned. "Hey, you-know-what calls. Got to go. Call me later if you need to."

"Take it easy." The connection was broken.

Neshi sat in his apartment, his mind blank. The reality of what was happening gave him mental overload, forcing all thought out, leaving nothing but blankness, which was probably his body's way of protecting him from collapse.

//

A day passed. He went about his normal routine, looking for more opportunities to gather information, to find whatever clues he could, and to pass these along to Ferene.

The two of them met for lunch at an open-air restaurant near TDH, where he told Ferene about Quintez's revelations.

"The government is murdering anyone they choose?" Ferene said, astonished. "They go into the streets and pick citizens at random—all to make sure the elite are serviced properly with organs when needed? Let me ask: does it seem logical that the bureaucrats need so *many* transplants?"

Neshi bit down hard on a bone. "Say that again," he said, ignoring the pain in his mouth.

"How often could the bureaucrats need something as specialized as transplants?"

Neshi reached forward and grabbed Ferene's wrist. "Are you suggesting that this indicates some sort of stepped-up schedule in the creation of that super race you were talking about?"

Zhrink-zhrink-zhrink.

The distinctive sound of Neshi's pager interrupted him. "Excuse me, Ferene," he said. "I'll be right back."

"Tech Detective Neshi, you had a call, but no message was left," the computer at TDH told him after he had used the restaurant calling box to tap into it.

"No clue?"

"Tech Detective Neshi, you had a call."

"Shut up," he said as he slammed the receiver down. He hurried back to the table Ferene and he were sharing.

"Anything important?" Ferene asked.

"Can't tell. Whoever it was hung up when the computer answered instead of me."

They talked for a bit longer, then Neshi decided to stop at his apartment before returning to the office. As he was unlocking the front door, he heard the telecaller and rushed inside to answer it. "Hello," he said. The connection was not a good one. "Who's this?"

"Neshi!"

It was Quintez.

"Don't say anything," the familiar voice commanded. "Just meet me in one hour at Moor's Edge. Near the gate."

"Okay," Neshi tried to say as nonchalantly as possible. "See you soon." Neshi had no idea what was going on, but he realized that he had to be at Moor's Edge as Quintez had asked.

*   *   *

The location was the city's equivalent of a slum. The buildings weren't just ancient, as in Old Town, they were dilapidated, as well. The streets were dirty, with fecal material making it necessary to step very carefully.

Leading down the center of that section of the city was a canal, one end originating at the municipal refuse center, the other leading into the moors. The canal was really a long cesspool, the top of it covered by a series of pipes from which chemicals poured continually over the sludge. Over the pipes was a plastic shield that kept most of the odor from escaping.

But not all of it.

The fumes that escaped combined with the other odors, making any visit to that location strictly a last-resort proposition.

Moor's Edge was at the very end of the pipeline, a nickname within TDH for the worst section of an already abysmal place. It was separated from the moors by a high wall that ran the circumference of that entire section of the city.

Citizens lived there only if they could not make it elsewhere in the city. They were literally driven to eating scraps of garbage and sleeping in tottering buildings that frequently collapsed on them in the middle of the night.

The moors could be seen through the iron grating around the sides of the gate Quintez had mentioned. Quintez appeared out of the shadows as soon as Neshi approached.

"What's going on?" Neshi asked. "I thought you were arrested."

"It wasn't a real arrest."

"I don't understand."

"I was being enlisted."

"Enlisted for what?"

"To pose as an outlaw."

"To track down any organized group of them you could find?"

"No. To commit a certain number of murders."

Neshi was stunned. "For the organs?"

"Yes. That's why I knew so much about what is going on. They had already interviewed me."

"But why you? That's a big secret to be trusted with. Why not a Tech Detective such as myself?"

"Don't you know, Neshi? Don't you suspect anything about me?"

"What?"

"Look, Neshi. Look!" Quintez unbuttoned his shirt. In the middle of his chest was a square lid with a tiny handle on it. Quintez pulled the lid back, revealing gears and flashing lights and a network of wires.

"You're an android!"

"But a very special variety: one of a kind. The Natasians control all the other androids that have ever come off the assembly line. I've faked it over the years."

"But what made you this way?"

"Just another experiment of theirs gone wrong."

"But androids aren't experimental. At least not any-more."

"I am."

"I don't see how—"

"Neshi, I have a flesh-and-blood brain up here, not an electronic computer!" He tapped his head several times, but Neshi could scarcely believe what Quintez was trying to tell him. "I've pretended to be obedient, pretended to be a slave like the rest of the androids, doing everything they ask. But not this time!"

102

He reached out and grabbed Neshi's shoulders. "Neshi, they want to create a new race of beings! It's really an obsession with them. That's what this slaughtering of the innocent is all about, not just transplantation."

"Yes, Quintez, I know what they've been attempting."

"You do?"

"It came to me from a very good authority. Take my word for that."

Quintez's eyes darted from side to side. "But that's not the end of it, Neshi."

Quintez was becoming increasingly irrational, judging by the expression on his face, the movement of his hands, the tone of his voice.

Neshi pulled away in shock.

"They've done it before, Neshi. Out there." He pointed to the sky. "On more worlds than either of us could count. But despite the eons of time they've had, the whole thing's never turned out right for them. Something intrinsic to what they wanted to achieve has always eluded them, but they won't give up, no matter who has to die in the process! Even if they have to resort to something as bizarre as a metallic guinea pig."

Neshi tried to brush Quintez's words aside as mere ravings. "How can you expect me to accept all that?"

"But it's true, Neshi. You may think I am acting this way, saying these things, due to some kind of electronic overload. Yet you must believe me. You must know what is going on. You must make contact somehow with the rebel groups and alert them before this world of ours, once colonized with such hope, becomes—"

He saw Neshi's still skeptical expression.

Suddenly, in a motion so quick that his hands were a blur, he grabbed a small loose piece of concrete on the ground, slammed it against his temple, split the metal underneath, and then ripped the top of his head open. "A normal brain!" he said before he collapsed at Neshi's feet.

And it was that—pinkish, throbbing, partially submerged in once-protective fluids, but now open to the stench-filled air, housed in what amounted to a round metal casing, wires leading from it into the otherwise mechanical body.

Neshi bent down and raised Quintez's body slightly.

"You must realize something else if . . . you . . . do not hate them enough already for . . . what they . . . are doing to us, playing with us . . . like hapless toys in the hands of monsters. You must realize that Etarina was one of the victims of their insatiable hunt for organs. She was . . . killed not by Jerusalemites or in a random foray by a lawless street gang but . . . her murderers were hired bounty hunters paid by the Natasians at a time years ago when . . . the official avenues of gaining organs had been . . . fluctuating unacceptably."

He could hardly be heard now.

"And I refused to stoop to that level. I broke away from them, Neshi. As you surely must."

Amazingly, he managed to stand, pushing Neshi aside. Sparks were flying out of the top of his head, from his ears, and also from his mouth. He staggered, but there was no cry of pain, which was the eeriest part of it, no sound at all but the *sizzle-sizzle-sizzle* of overloaded electrical circuits going haywire.

He fell forward, his weight extreme, his outward look of skinniness deceptive, landing on the plastic covering of the canal directly below, splintering it into uncountable shards, and falling into the putrescent mess beneath, his body immediately covered with chemicals, the acids within them eating off the veneer of lifelike plasticoat skin, revealing metal frame and tubing and tiny lights that flashed briefly and then went dark. In seconds whatever was left was swept along over the edge and into the literal wasteland of the moors.

Neshi stumbled as he tried to stand. His first reaction, his first compelling desire, was to get weapons and ammunition and blow up TDH and everyone in it. But he would surely perish as well. And what he knew about the government, about the work of Tech Detectives such as himself, about the countless other invaluable details of a functioning law enforcement subculture, would be indispensable to the Jerusalemites.

Neshi managed to stand without tottering, managed to beat down his initial irrational reaction born out of the intensity of his anger.

I must contact Ferene, he told himself. *How can I return to TDH and play the game of pretending while knowing what I do?*

He ran from that place, from its foul odors and its decay, into the center of the city and toward his apartment.

Neshi encountered crowds on the way back. Dusk had just started to fall, and an early evening walk could be quite pleasant. Crimes generally weren't inflicted on large numbers of citizens; it was those alone or in couples who would have the greatest to fear.

He must have been uncommonly high-strung, even bizarre in his behavior, because he caused males as well as females to turn and look questioningly in his direction as he passed by.

He came upon a public rest facility and entered. As soon as he stood before one of the reflective surfaces, he saw why he had caused the reaction. He looked as though he

had been on an all-night drinking spree: clothes dishev-
eled, face smudged with dirt, deep circles under his eyes,
and blood on the backs of both hands. Apparently while
he had been holding Quintez, he had scratched himself.

He knew he had to clean himself up before entering the
apartment building, so he took some towels, soaked them
in water, and washed his face clean. Then he rinsed his
hands. The cuts weren't deep and would heal nicely.

He straightened his clothes as best as he could and
looked at his reflection once more.

Etarina!

In the back of his mind rested the surety that the image
was some sort of emotion-induced hallucination, but this
analysis was momentarily swept aside by the seeming reality of viewing her face in the mirror instead of his own.

He reached out and touched the slick surface of the
polished glass reflection.

"Etar—" he said out loud, only to see the vision become
that of the hunchback, yet more grotesque this time, the
top of the head open and—

For one of the very few times in his life, a scream ripped
from his lips.

"They murdered you!" he yelled a split second later.
"As far as they were concerned, you were just another
carcass to use in their scientific games. There was no
thought given to the pain you endured, the pain inflicted
on me and others who knew you, who saw how kind and
loving and wonderful you had been before they got hold
of you."

He took a waste cylinder and slammed it against the
glass, which shattered on contact. Then he wrenched the
washing bowls from their hinges, sending water spouting

out of the jagged ends of pipes. Finally, his energy spent, he sank to the floor and wept uncontrollably.

Just then a male came in. "Tech Detective, are you ill?" the short, stocky individual asked, and then, recognizing him, added, "Say, aren't you the one who tracked down that awful hunchback?"

Neshi stood, his cheeks wet with tears. "The hunchback couldn't help herself," he said, his voice rising. "She wasn't responsible for her actions."

"She? The hunchback was a female?" the citizen said, startled.

"Yes. Despite what you have heard from the media," Neshi said as he grabbed him by the collar. "Her mind was corrupted along with her body. They did it to her—those monsters we call the Natasians. She was a victim, as all of us will be if we don't do something about it, soon."

He let go. The citizen was shaking with fear.

"Forgive me," Neshi said as he hurried out of the rest facility, leaving the citizen standing there looking dumbfoundedly at the not inconsequential wreckage spread out in front of him.

A block away from the apartment building, Neshi saw three TDH airmobiles in front of it. Half a dozen fellow Tech Detectives gathered next to them. It was obvious that they were looking for him. Once they entered his apartment, they would find the missing tape.

Then reports would come in of his bizarre behavior in public. Very little else would be needed to justify placing him under corrective confinement, a nondescript label hiding a quite effective and horrifying form of brainwashing reserved for Tech Detectives who, in the judgment of their superiors, had "gone wrong" or showed every sign of doing so. Part of the treatment involved a brain-wave re-structuring that, if applied properly, eliminated "counter-productive memories," leaving only those that made the patient a good Tekkie once again.

Which would render him useless to the Jerusalemites!

If he could gain access to TDH, do at least some kind of damage, and arrange to meet Ferene afterward at the catacombs—

He stopped in a telecall booth, dialed in his Tekkie Code, and called Ferene at home.

Ferene picked up the receiver immediately. Neshi told him what was happening.

"It's got to be now!" Ferene declared. "We cannot linger. I'll go on ahead. Meet me there as soon as you can."

"Fine," Neshi said. "And good-bye."

"I pray, my friend, that our farewell will only be temporary."

12

Storyteller let out a big sigh. "Time for a break," he said.

"No, no!" the crowd protested in unison.

One of those present stood. "Storyteller, please go on. We want to know what happens to this Neshi and how he carries out his plan to help the Jerusalemites."

"And the meaning of the visions experienced by certain Jerusalemites," added another. "We are confused. Please help us."

Storyteller nodded with resignation. "Fine, my friends," he said at last. "We continue."

The others let out a shout of approval.

"Neshi is successful in implanting a so-called computer virus in the central unit at TDH, which is linked with all the other TDH units throughout the planet. A computer virus is an electronic command, completely unknown to anybody but the one responsible, with a special code that is his alone. When activated, it begins a destructive rampage throughout all the records stored in that computer and then, eventually, in any others with which it is linked. It is like an electronic cancer, attacking normal files and rendering them useless."

"Then what?" several asked, their curiosity unbounded.

"As he attempts to leave, he is spotted by a suspicious fellow Tekkie who pursues him. Before long, Neshi is trapped, surrounded by a group of Tekkies.

"They at first verbally abuse Neshi for betraying the honor of the corps, calling him the worst sort of traitor. Then they beat him into unconsciousness.

"In the meantime, Ferene and some other undercover Jerusalemite comrades have been alerted to the circumstances and stealthily follow the vehicle into which Neshi has been thrown."

"What then, Storyteller? What happens to Neshi next?"

"He awakens in an unknown location."

13

His eyelids felt as though they had been welded shut. As he tried to open them, bursts of pain ricocheted through his brain in thin little slivers, one right after the other, until the consciousness to which he had just returned threatened to dissipate once again.

Finally he fought past the pain, determined to open his eyes and see where he had been confined.

It was a bare room—no windows, only a heavy metal door with a single square of thick, shatterproof glass at eye level—stark white, with a curved ceiling, a single light for illumination. No toilet facilities, no chair, no bed, just the four walls, the floor, the ceiling, and that door.

The silence was total, except for the sound of his breathing, raspy at times as pain tore around his ribs, down his back, in his elbows and knees.

There were no mirrors, so he couldn't examine his face, but he was quite certain he had two black eyes, at least half a dozen bruises, and lips that were cut and very sore.

He walked haltingly to the door. He could barely see the corridor, not very far down it either way. Only featureless walls greeted him.

Perhaps it was the sense of oppressive isolation that got to him first, of not knowing where he was, of being in a sinister cocoon, indeed perhaps more than the pain each time he blinked, the soreness of his throat as he swallowed.

"Take this medicine, traitor."

The words flashed into his mind like a burst of lightning across a darkened sky.

"We're going to clean you out and fill you up again our way."

He must have been semiconscious part of the time, some receptacle of his brain storing isolated sentences and spewing them up at random.

"When we get done with you, you'll hate the very name they use."

"No, I won't. Don't forget my other training. I'm stronger than you think."

"When we're through, if we asked you to do so, you would shoot your own mother."

"No! No! That's wicked. That's evil!"

"Do not deceive yourself with those words. There is no such thing, no good or evil. What is, is."

"You murdered Etarina."

"So what?"

He had blacked out momentarily and at first couldn't perceive what had brought him back to awareness. And

112

then he saw. The door had swung open, making a *swooshing* sound in the process.

He approached it, grabbing at one mental straw, the only one he could find. Perhaps he was being rescued. Perhaps the door was controlled from a central panel and had been unlocked by Ferene or another Jerusalemite.

Neshi entered the corridor. On his left, at the very end, was a door. He hurried toward it, turned the knob. It opened!

He went into the room on the other side.

A dozen lab technicians were standing at tables or talking to one another. On the three tables were bits and pieces of—

"No!" he screamed out loud. "This is monstrous."

They turned, looked at him, and smiled.

He ran up to the nearest one and shook him. "You can't play with lives this way, rearrange bodies, taking a brain from one citizen and putting it in another. What of the consequences? Do you *know?*"

The technician grabbed him by the neck, lifted him up, and flung him across the room. He landed against a white cabinet with glass doors that shattered in every direction.

The room spun. He shook his head. At the opposite end was a window.

Several of the technicians saw where he was looking. "A very nice window!" they exclaimed in unison. "Can we give you a helping hand?" another added.

They approached as he tried to scramble to his feet.

"Here, take my hand," one said, smirking, as he pulled out his left arm from its socket and threw it at him.

An android!

The arm and hand glanced off his cheek, gouging out a piece of skin. Every technician in the room was laughing hysterically at him. "It's nighttime now," someone said. "My eyes were manufactured to see in the dark. You can borrow them, if you like." The technician ripped his eyes out, bent down, and handed them to Neshi. In the sockets were loose wires and metal receptacles where the plastic orbs had been.

"I can hear better, too!" another added.

"I can smell odors at a distance of miles," said a third technician.

They gathered around him.

"Take a piece of each one of us with you."

He finally got to his feet, fueled by adrenaline, and used the training that had been pounded into him at the academy. In a matter of seconds, he had cut a path through the synthetic metal bodies, sending them sprawling in every direction.

The window. So close. He had to get away, even if it meant his death. They must never be allowed to carve any secrets out of him. They must never find out about Ferene or—

The androids were getting to their feet, arms outstretched, advancing toward him.

There was no choice.

He jumped through the window, the glass shattering, chill night air against his face, tall moor grass like very large whips stinging his flesh, brackish water splashing as he hit the surface, his mouth filling up with the awful stuff. Then came the sounds of laser pistols sending their beams through the air, a technician framed in a halo of fire and sparks tumbling forward out of the window . . . hands grabbing Neshi, lifting him, pressing down on his lungs, the water spurting out of his mouth.

Just before his eyes closed, he dimly perceived a hovering figure and let loose a barely audible cry of surprise and relief.

"Ferene!"

And as though echoing down a long tunnel, just before unconsciousness, a becalming tide swept over him. *"Neshi, listen, you're not going to die. You're not going to die."*

14

Neshi knew he was in Moor's Edge even before he opened his eyes. The now-familiar odors acted as a kind of atomizing scent, and his own coughing awakened him.

Ferene was sitting beside him. Standing at his feet were two rough-looking individuals attired in furry garb.

His head was resting on a crumpled-up piece of rubber-like padding. He felt a residue of pain from his brief flirtation with corrective confinement.

"You would not have survived very much longer," Ferene said softly.

"I thought I was tough enough to take anything," he replied ironically.

"After they beat you, if they were true to form, they stuffed you full of hallucinatory drugs," Ferene said.

Neshi told them what he thought he had seen in the

room down the corridor from his cell. "It never happened?" he asked.

"Probably not."

"But those laser blasts. I saw one of the androids in flames."

"That wasn't an android. What you saw was one of your fellow Tekkies."

Neshi fell silent, the vision of that burning form more stark in retrospect.

"It shows how badly drugs can be abused," Ferene added. "You are hardly as susceptible as someone without the benefit of your rigorous training. Think of what happens to the poor innocent citizen who is wrongfully convicted and subjected to the nightmare you faced. Very few survive as more than pitiful shells of what they once were."

Ferene rubbed his chin, then asked, "You got out rather easily, wouldn't you say?"

Neshi had to admit that his friend was right. "That seems strange," he mused. "Their security measures are better than that. It should have taken a real struggle."

"Indeed."

One of the two other apparent Jerusalemites broke their silence. "If Tech Detective Neshi is now able to join us, we should hasten off," he said, his gentle tone the antithesis of his rough manner.

Neshi looked about, his eyes confirming the location to which his sense of smell had alerted him.

"Not a glorious place for a revolution to begin, is it?" Ferene asked ironically.

"You started banding together here?"

"Yes. A long time ago. Moor's Edge has been written off for years, as you know."

"My friends," the same Jerusalemite said again, reminding them.

"Yes, I know," Ferene acknowledged. "Can you make it, Neshi?"

Neshi nodded. "I don't see that any of us has a universe of choices at the moment."

So they left Moor's Edge through a jagged archway that had been eaten into the outer wall by wood-consuming vermin.

Half a mile away were the catacombs.

Less than five minutes after they had entered the ancient cave site, an explosion sealed the entrances.

"What the—" Neshi began, startled.

"To prevent any possibility that we would be followed," Ferene told him.

Neshi smiled in appreciation. "There is no turning back," he whispered.

"Not for any of us."

Ferene and he looked back at the tunnel behind them, cloudy with the dust of ten million years. For an instant they saw the ancient bones of an unknown colonist tumble from a carved-out portion of the old rock wall and shatter as they hit the ground. White powder was all that was now left.

15

Thousands of Jerusalemites were gathered in the huge crater, which seemed much like an amphitheater formed by one of the meteors that hit the planet once every thousand years or so. Gnarled tree branches formed a natural ceiling, so thickly overgrown that they provided shelter from any government patrols.

Neshi, Ferene, and their guides reached the site by traveling a network of tunnels just beyond the last of the burial places at the catacombs. It was a journey that took nearly a day of very hard travel, since the tunnels were often not tall enough to allow them to stand up straight. And there was very little air, just enough to keep them from suffocating, but too little for them to walk more than a brief distance without resting.

Fortunately the Jerusalemite guides had brought along some food—dried fruits and vegetables, primarily. Water was plentiful in the tunnels, collecting in clear pools every few miles, fed by underground streams.

"Our world, our home," Neshi said softly. "What has become of it when we must go through all this in order to obtain justice and freedom and throw off the yoke of the—"

"Natasians!" one of the guides interrupted.

"Indeed, the Natasians," Neshi agreed. "I look forward to meeting them one day face-to-face and—"

Both of the guides started laughing.

Then the one who had spoken walked over to Neshi and Ferene. "My name is Yanif. Please forgive the rudeness." He turned to Ferene. "Have you not told him?"

"No. I didn't want to burden my friend with an overload of knowledge, any one component of which he would need time to assimilate."

"I can understand that. But I think one as important as Tech Detective Neshi should not have any surprises from now on."

Ferene nodded in reluctant agreement. "Neshi, you probably will never meet the Natasians, at least in the usual sense of the term," Ferene said slowly.

"I don't understand what you are trying to tell me."

"The Natasians don't exist."

"What are you saying?" Neshi asked, beginning to doubt Ferene's grasp of reality.

"The Natasians don't exist as flesh-and-blood beings."

"What Ferene is saying," Yanif broke in, "is that they exist only as invisible beings of pure spirit, with no physical form or substance."

Neshi simply could not speak at first. What had he gotten himself involved in now? Were the Jerusalemites merely deranged?

"All this control, decades of pulling the strings of government, and yet they have no bodies?" Neshi mused out loud, almost absentmindedly, his thoughts whirling.

"They've been working through representatives of our race," Yanif said. "Until we were able to discern the truth, all of us were puppets tied to their strings."

Yanif grabbed him by the shoulders. "And it hasn't been decades, as far as the power of the Natasians is concerned, though that is what the doctored records would lead you to believe. Neshi, they have been here since the very beginning."

Neshi broke away, looking frantically from Yanif to Ferene to the other Jerusalemite.

"How can I believe all this?" he screamed. "You are as crazed as the creatures of the moors who attack the unsuspecting. And I am no wiser than their victims for venturing here with you and becoming vulnerable at your hands."

"But to what would you propose to return now?" Ferene asked.

Weakness from the beating and the drugs confused his thoughts, robbing him of the mental clarity that was a hallmark of all Tekkies, especially him.

Ferene stood directly in front of his friend. "Neshi. Neshi, we all have been under a delusion, you know. For every one of us, it has been a time of oppression, Natasian oppression. Please do not categorize us as mad. That is why I wanted the truth to be given to you in stages, so you would not suffer a kind of intellectual regurgitation. You are the only Tech Detective we have ever been able to talk to like this."

Tears were forming in Ferene's eyes. "I became a Jerusalemite because of losing two very close friends to the

Natasians. The loss itself haunted me, very much so, but it was also *how* they died."

Neshi's emotions were subsiding a bit as Ferene's were gathering momentum. He had never seen his friend so highly charged.

"How did they die?" he asked with utmost gentleness.

"They were sacrificed on altars of metal and plastic in a ceremony dedicated to the worship of the Natasians' leader."

Neshi was quite amazed that he had never thought of the Natasians as having a leader.

Ferene was beginning to pace frenziedly.

"Their hearts were cut out and offered up to—" The words choked in his throat. "But first their tongues were pulled out so they could only cry in anguish without being able to plead for mercy. And then their hearts. And then—"

"Please, Ferene," Yanif begged him. "Please. You're going to do yourself harm."

"Then harm it is!" Ferene shouted. "It is harm that will mend. It is pain that will stop. But for my friends there was nothing of the sort. They could not recover. Their lives were ripped from them by those whom the Natasians had—"

He was starting to babble but fought off any attempt to calm him down.

"*Possessed!*" He spit out the word.

"Possessed?" Neshi said, puzzling over the meaning of what Ferene was saying.

"Yes! Taken over—their minds, their bodies, their very essence!"

In an instant, stunning in its suddenness, his manner changed, control returning just when it seemed most unattainable. "You know whom the Natasians chose to do the deed?"

Neshi shook his head.

"Children, Neshi. Innocent little children. Males and females under the age of ten. Each held a dagger, each plunged it into my friends, and each carved those frail, frail bodies apart like the carcasses of dumb beasts."

"But how could you know all this?"

"Because, Neshi, I know."

"But how could you?" Neshi reeled under the impact of his suspicions.

"I do!" Ferene said, his voice suddenly very weak. "It was two decades ago. Oh, Neshi, I know every detail, every bloody, awful detail *because I was one of the children holding one of those daggers!*"

They walked much of the rest of the distance in silence. Ferene was unwilling or unable to fill in any more details, but Neshi could conjecture well enough. The Natasians gained control of the children from an early age and attempted total ownership of each so that any will, any desire, any act was not that of the individual but of the Natasians themselves.

Neshi admired, in a perverse way, the masterful nature of the Natasian plan. With attention would have come scrutiny. Now they could do whatever they planned in the breeding ground of the public's ignorance. Cancer undetected was the most dangerous of all!

And yet what was he to make of the claim that the Natasians were not flesh-and-blood beings but rather some insubstantial entities, perhaps like whirling vapors? Surely Ferene and Yanif had referred to the influence of the Natasians, not their actual personification?

Less than an hour from the crater, Neshi hesitantly approached his friend and asked him what he had meant.

"Exactly what I said," Ferene replied, not breaking stride, "without ambiguity."

"But it is inconceivable," Neshi persisted. "Only that which we can see and touch and hear has validity."

"That is what we have been taught as a race over the millions of years of our habitation here on this planet. But it is not the truth, Neshi. What has been force-fed us by those benefiting from the maintenance of our delusions is not at all what life is all about, nor has it ever been!"

He stopped for a few seconds before continuing. "What you will soon see will cause much of what you had thought to be factual and real and proper and true to evaporate as though it had never existed, even for an instant."

Neshi could see that the subject was closed, at least as far as Ferene was concerned.

16

Thousands of Jerusalemites had dug out little places to sit around the walls of the huge crater. Neshi was overwhelmed by their sheer number. "Where have they all come from?" he whispered to Ferene.

"These males and females have been gathering together for a very long time. They are the so-called criminals that you and the other Tech Detectives have been called upon to hunt down over the years."

"But I seldom let any criminal slip through my fingers."

"That may have been what you thought. Let me ask you this: how many did you actually bring back with you?"

"Very few. They often had to be chased quite a distance. It was impractical to carry their bodies for any period of time."

"So you let them stay where they fell."

"Yes." Neshi thought he caught Ferene's drift. "But I

checked each one. There was no heartbeat. There were no brain waves. They were dead!"

Ferene took a small white pill out of a pocket in his uniform. "This is a remarkable little item, Neshi. It can cause the illusion of death."

"They weren't dead then?"

"Many of them only seemed to be so. Of course, when they were blasted through the heart or strangled or drowned, the signs of death were real. But not otherwise."

"And the effects of that pill wore off and the numbers of the Jerusalemites grew?"

"Precisely. You are the best of the Tech Detectives, of course, but multiply your caseload by the thousands of others in the city we've just left and in many more around the planet, and do this over a period of decades, and you can see that the escaped criminals alone could number a huge total."

"By the natural process of procreation, the figures could grow astronomically. But where could they hide?" Suddenly Neshi had figured it out and provided the answer himself. "Underground." That was all he said. But it was enough.

Even though the Natasians were supposed to be spirit beings, that did not mean they were also omnipresent. At least Neshi failed to see how that could ever be so.

"That is only the tip of the iceberg, if you will. Neshi, you have no idea," Ferene added, "what a world, a way of life has been existing down there all these years. The catacombs—places of death—ironically masking a growing army dedicated to the beginning of a new life on this planet, free of the Natasian yoke!"

Neshi and Ferene were standing just out of sight of the gathered Jerusalemites, in a tunnel leading out into the crater. But Neshi could see enough of them to be filled with a growing sense of wonderment. Decades below the surface in conditions that were hardly the stuff of luxury and ease. Cold and dark and often cramped, waiting for the moment when their mission would spring them forth.

Some were quite rough looking, armed with spiked metallic clubs, clothed in the skins of wild animals. A few, in striking contrast, were clean shaven, wearing the uniforms of bureaucrats but now standing in allegiance to a new order that would attempt to overthrow the old as quickly as possible.

They all were on their feet, singing an anthemlike melody that stirred a flow of adrenaline within Neshi that he had never felt before.

"What are they waiting for?" Neshi asked.

Ferene, Yanif, and the other Jerusalemite who had made the journey from the catacombs all turned and looked at him.

"Tell me, what are they waiting here for?" he repeated, thinking they had not heard him.

"It's not *what*, my friend," Ferene said. "It's *who*."

He could not, no matter how desperately he tried, avoid their gaze. He could not ignore the implications of what they were telling him. "But I have not been one of you. I have not sacrificed for you."

"You have given up more than you know."

"But what about those whose dedication has been manifested by decades of deprivation, of waiting, of planning?"

"For you, Neshi. It has all been because of you."

"I—I can't accept that."

"We've had confidence that someone would come to

join us, to lead us, to capture what we've never had but now can take from those who've denied us all along."

"But how do you *know*?"

"Because of other prophecies given to us by our beloved Yuane."

It is the Day of Armageddon. A field of blood spreads out before me. It is several feet deep. Bodies lie on the ground, sometimes piled high on top of one another, stretching on to the distant horizon, the arms of the dying held up for mercy and then cut down like wheat reaped at harvest.

Neshi looked out at the thousands of expectant warriors, untrained soldiers ready for the battle of their lives. "But how much time is there?" he asked. "What plans have been made?"

"We have very little time," Yanif answered. "We need to mount an attack by next week."

"Surely you are jesting?"

Their expressions said otherwise.

"But what about planning?" He sensed that there was something else, something that necessitated the seeming absurdity of what Yanif had just told him. "Departure Date is next week, isn't it?"

"It is," Ferene replied.

"Where?"

"At Asframore."

Asframore, the almost fabled central command headquarters for the entire planet, long rumored to be at one location or another. Few knew where it actually was, and even Tech Detectives weren't in that favored group.

"But can we find it in time?" he asked.

"We *have* found it," Ferene told him. "The question is whether or not we can *reach* it in time."

"Where, Ferene?"

130

"A journey that would take nine days under the best of circumstances. And we have only seven days under the *worst* of circumstances."

The crowd was becoming even louder, bordering on unruly.

"They await their leader," Yanif said.

Their leader.

The word reverberated in his mind, intruding upon his protestations. "I am unworthy," he said feebly.

"But are you unwilling?" Ferene asked.

"Go out and talk to them. I must ask that, Ferene," he pleaded. "I need a little time. Just a little."

"I can mollify them for five minutes, no more," Ferene acknowledged.

Neshi nodded and went off by himself.

It should be during sleeptime, of course.

Those words from that plastic fragment filtered back into his mind. If the so-called Departure Date was not short-circuited, then millions would die; he was convinced of that. They would get into their sleep cylinders, pull down the lids over them, and never awaken again, the end coming in a quiet cessation of life as fluids of death entered their pores.

Neshi had no idea how the mixture of previously sedating fluids would be adjusted, but males and females, young and old, would end up climbing into their own coffins.

There were a hundred centers of life on the planet, a hundred metropolises, each in the midst of a very inhospitable region surrounded by moors or adjacent to large wooded areas in which lived creatures of dread. Every single city was connected to Asframore by a network of computers and other remote-control apparatuses.

The rationale for withholding the location of Asframore from the general populace was that dissident groups would be thwarted in any attempt to create general havoc. These might plague individual cities but never the central command center of the government.

But what was Departure Date all about?

"Neshi, please." Ferene's voice interrupted his thoughts. "The moment is now. It cannot last forever."

Neshi recalled the stories about the very early years of life on the planet. Eventually the harshness had been tamed to a degree, cities springing up in the midst of the moors, survival carved from an inhospitable place. There was expectation of a future of peace and surpassing progress once the elements no longer needed to be feared.

But something had changed. There had been a turning point, next to impossible to pin down, but real nevertheless—a watershed in the history of that world. Something had torn away the vaunting promise and brought the tragic reality of the present: a long-entrenched dictatorship fostered by an unknown group.

It had gone on for countless centuries of the planet's history, this mockery of what once was. Ferene and Yanif were correct. It could go on no longer, Neshi told himself as he stepped out into the crater and a roar of approval arose from the multitude awaiting his appearance.

"We begin now an odyssey from which there is no turning back."

He had not prepared what he would say, but the words flowed forth with breathtaking fluidity, some part of his inner self opening up as never before.

"We do not want to retreat," someone from the crowd shouted. "We want to march forward."

"And that we will do," Neshi responded, "for the sake of justice and in pursuit of victory."

He would say only what he felt to be honest, and the crowd knew that. They accepted the truth of what he called the long nightmare of the centuries giving them only a week to turn back the onslaught or be drowned by this last, awful swelling tidal wave of destruction, sweeping away any who stood in its path, impotent and unprepared.

That night, after two hours of exhortation, he would lie down on a rock shelf and try to sleep, both dreading the time ahead for its expected rigors and scarcely able to wait for the challenge to begin.

17

The odyssey to Asframore was a circuitous route, most of it underground, through the network of tunnels that apparently honeycombed the entire planet.

A few scouts volunteered for surface duty, the most hazardous job of all. Contact with them was maintained through some very powerful stolen portable radasonic units capable of sending signals through the air or thousands of feet of earth. Set on a coded frequency calibrated by Neshi with utmost care, there was no way the signals could be detected, let alone deciphered.

If the underground tunnels had been in a straight line, they could have made it to Asframore in less than three days, but there were constant twists and turns. More than once, they had to refer to maps that an advance party had made weeks before in a trial run.

"Ferene, how did you discover the location of Asframore?" Neshi asked at one point.

"It really was quite by accident," the Jerusalemite commented. "One of our exploratory parties came back with a report so bizarre it could only have been a description of Asframore." He leaned over to Neshi and whispered conspiratorially. "One of them apparently got too close. What he experienced drove him quite mad for a while."

"Do the others know?"

"Oh, they do. But I don't want to remind them of it just now."

"What will protect us from the same fate?"

"We have been alerted, Neshi. Madness intrudes more easily on the unsuspecting."

That was correct, of course; they knew in a general sense what was ahead. And they could expect just about anything as far as the Natasians were concerned.

Day one passed without mishap, though not without delay and more than a little discomfort, the thin, humid air making numerous rest stops mandatory. Frequent wrong turns, despite the maps, required the retracing of many steps, but they made it through that day in reasonably good shape, and at night, or what they calculated to be night with the aid of the scouts aboveground, they sat and talked for a bit and then fell asleep.

As Neshi's eyes closed, he recalled some earlier moments that day with Ferene.

"Ours is a plan conceived by the wisdom of more than one of us," Ferene had said. "Asframore is in the center of a large lake. Surrounding it on the shore is a force field three stories high, rather like the one in the arena but not nearly as vulnerable. In the lake itself are meat-eating fish of a particularly voracious sort. The water itself is poisonous to all life but the fish."

"You paint a most optimistic picture, my friend," Neshi had said facetiously.

"That is as far as our knowledge goes," Ferene had continued. "We can only assume that there are all manner of armaments inside Asframore. But we do know this one additional detail: the tunnels run under the place, and the Natasians are not aware of them. They have gotten into the rut of thinking themselves all-powerful, ignoring the possibility that any other group could ever be smart enough to figure out a way of getting into Asframore from the outside, never realizing that the route with the best chance of success is underneath!"

"They are manifesting an impregnability mentality."

"Precisely. That is the weak link in their chain."

But as the next day proved, the Jerusalemites were to face more than one weak link of their own.

18

The ceiling of the tunnel had collapsed. The planet was subject to earthquakes, the suspected cause of the barrier of rock and dirt before them.

"But according to the maps, in this particular area, there is just no other way," Yanif observed nervously. "What are we going to do?"

"Dig," Neshi said simply.

"Yes, of course. But how long will it take?"

"We'll find out when we finish."

Yanif stood there, embarrassed by the obviousness of the answer. Shaking his head in a self-deprecatory fashion, he became the first one to start removing the barrier.

The heat had not dissipated a single degree. Even the most rugged among them—a large percentage of the total, to be sure—found the combination of humidity and hard labor nearly unbearable.

"I never want to see another pile of rocks," one of them said.

"Except the ones you carry around in that fat head of yours," jested another Jerusalemite.

Finally the way was nearly cleared and they could see past the few rocks that remained. The collapse of the ceiling had not been caused by a quake but by a creature building a nest for its loathsome offspring. Instead of using branches and soft moss, the mother had found rocks to be satisfactory nesting material.

They stood in shocked silence at the sight of the babies: long serpentine creatures, their skin a dark oily looking brown, large eyes on stalks jutting out from the tops of their nearly flat heads that tapered down to bumpy snouts and mouths that stretched from one end of those heads to the other. Even though obviously just recently born, their teeth were already well-formed, narrow and jagged, and very, very sharp looking.

"We have to kill them," Neshi said. "We can't bypass them. We certainly can't pick them up and deposit them elsewhere. And we can't trust their goodwill and agreeable disposition and simply step over them." He turned to Ferene and Yanif. "Agreed?"

"Agreed."

The creatures did not die quickly. Though terribly young, they were not especially weak and all eight of them made an effort to ward off their attackers.

The weapons used couldn't be sonic in nature for fear of causing further collapse, so they had to use fire-throwers first, then shovels to finish the job.

It was messy and unexpectedly poignant as one of the

creatures moved in front of a sibling to protect it and the others showed a tendency to band together for the protection of the group.

Our babies are so helpless after three or four years or more, Neshi thought. *However ghastly they seem, these creatures put our offspring to shame when it comes to such a basic matter as defending themselves.*

The job was done.

"Wait!" exclaimed Yanif. "This one's still alive!"

The Jerusalemite stood over it with a shovel. The creature's two eyes vibrated with pain and fear as it tried frantically to crawl away. And then its mouth opened and its long reptilian tongue jutted outward. At the very tip was a piece of food that it apparently had been holding for imminent digestion. It laid this on the ground directly in front of it.

"It's offering me something to eat," Yanif said in amazement. "It's trying to buy its life." Yanif dropped the shovel, touched by the gesture, and reached out his hand. The creature lunged forward, sinking its long teeth into Yanif's proffered hand and then chewing along his arm to the elbow. Yanif fell back in agony. In just three seconds the creature had reached his shoulder.

Neshi took a laser knife and cut apart its temple, then severed the head from the body, taking Yanif's arm with it.

The Jerusalemite was nearly unconscious, having lost a startling amount of blood in less than a minute.

Neshi and Ferene bent down beside him.

"Please go on," he said, his voice scarcely audible. "Conquer Asframore for me and millions of others who have died over the years." Yanif was gone then, his eyelids closing, his mouth dropping open in the frozen look of death that came with unbearable pain.

They covered his body and went on their way until they came face-to-face with the worst nightmare any of them had ever encountered: the mother.

19

None of those in Neshi and Ferene's group knew there was any lingering menace from the encounter just experienced. After all, however important because of Neshi's presence, it was nevertheless one single group out of several going off in as many directions with the ultimate intention of reaching Asframore and surrounding it—one group coming in from the north, another from the south, a third from the east, a fourth from the west. For the thousands massed at the crater to have gone only in one huge group would have taken far longer than the time allowed them, and if they were discovered by the Natasians, they would have presented a single target in a single place.

In no way were they prepared for an onslaught that had little or nothing to do with their enemy of record.

The first Jerusalemite was killed less than half an hour

after the infant creatures had been killed. He was at the very end of the line. The mother came around a corner unseen and wrapped her mouth around his head, preventing him from screaming as she quickly dragged him off.

But he was missed within seconds. "Getran has disappeared!" a man named Urnak said as he approached Neshi and Ferene after running up the line of Jerusalemites.

"No sign of him at all?" Neshi asked.

"No. Just gone!"

Within seconds someone else from the rear came forward with the same story. Then another. And another.

"Ferene, what in the world do we have here?" Neshi inquired of his friend.

"It cannot be that our enemy has discovered us," Ferene mused out loud.

Someone came running toward them, flailing his arms. "It lashes out from the darkness and then is gone!" he was shouting.

"*What* does this, soldier?" Neshi grabbed him, demanding an answer.

"Their mother, I think. Yes, it's their mother, avenging their deaths!"

Ferene called Neshi aside. "We have ventured into the path of a creature who has probably been living here for more centuries than we shall ever know. That's the one thing we failed to reckon with in our planning, Neshi. We are headed toward the central point, the hub of the Natasians' domain, but we have set foot in the domain of a species that could slaughter us all."

"You think the mother could enlist others of her kind?" Neshi's question felt like ice in his throat.

Ferene never got a chance to answer. Suddenly, from

144

the darkness, which was lit only enough to show their own bodies and their path ahead by a few feet, shapes sprang out of nowhere, slithery beings with eyes on long stalks and sharp, jagged teeth, attacking those utterly unprepared for it.

The Jerusalemites fought back, using their laser weapons to slice up their attackers, but in fact there were vast hordes of the creatures, their bodies piling higher and higher.

Neshi found himself cut off from the Jerusalemites in a little alcove. A huge creature, certainly larger than the others he had glimpsed, stood in front of him.

The mother!

It spit at him, an action so quick that he couldn't even fire his pistol before a stream of yellowish fluid hit his cheek. Instantly his nerve ends began to vibrate with unimaginable pain. He tried to stay on his feet, tried to raise the pistol, but strength was leaving his body rapidly. He fell to his knees, looking up briefly as the mother creature slithered up to him, towering over him.

He vaguely heard someone yelling and saw the creature stumble to one side, a spiked metallic club stuck in the back of its head. It was spitting more bursts of the fluid out but not hitting anyone in its dying frenzy. Finally it collided against the rock wall and fell into a lifeless pile.

Neshi's mind was exploding with agony. He could hardly see Ferene, could hardly hear his friend's frantic plea: "Swallow this liquid. It is an antidote, I hope the *right* one. Swallow it!"

"Give . . . whatever . . . you . . . have . . . to the others," he managed to say in choking gasps.

"*No!*" Ferene shouted. "If you don't survive, we lose them anyway. Having you die is like ripping the heart out of each and every one of them. They are prepared to sacrifice their lives, but not if you have thrown away your own."

Neshi sipped from a little silver flask. Within a few seconds its effects were apparent, the pain dissipating, his strength beginning to return after a minute or so.

"When you first showed them to me," he said in a raspy whisper, "I never realized how handy these little things would be."

Ferene smiled, obviously relieved and rejoicing. "As we all have just found out," Ferene remarked, "there is much that no one can anticipate."

20

The scouts were sending down a report that the structure in front of them seemed quite natural, hewn by the forces of nature over the centuries—but it was not. There was one obvious indication of this: its exceptional height.

"It appears to almost touch the sky," a scout observed, "and it seems unfinished at the top, as though the Natasians, using flesh-and-blood slaves, were trying to build a tower to reach the outer universe itself."

Looking like an unnaturally tall, narrow volcanic mountain arising out of the midst of a large lake, it was nothing more than a cleverly conceived facade behind which, they assumed, was the command center for Natasian control of the entire planet.

The lake itself was inhabited by nameless species of creatures apparently imported from regions on the planet otherwise inhospitable to life. Every so often one or more could be seen poking their heads through the surface, then disappearing again, and the sight chilled the blood of the scouts.

"The element we have in our favor is the fact that they are unaware of the tunnels directly underneath," Neshi reminded Ferene. "Is everyone set?"

"Indeed, Neshi. The Natasians' attention is going to be focused on the aboveground attack, which will be only diversionary. The bulk of our forces are to come up from below, striking within the very guts of the fortress."

Neshi fell into silence, thinking about the Jerusalemites who would be sacrificing their lives during the coming battle. He would have hoped that it could be otherwise, but then a protracted series of attacks against the cities would have caused more casualties. Better to strike at the nerve center of Natasian control!

And strike they did. Hundreds of Jerusalemites were diverted above ground and attacked, sending rockets from handmade launchers all around the perimeter of Asframore. These got as far as the force field and exploded harmlessly.

Neshi and Ferene led the main thrust of the Jerusalemites beneath Asframore. At each turn in the winding network, they were prepared to encounter some surprise defensive device or strategy of which they had been unaware.

Nothing.

Even though he was relieved, Neshi felt growing apprehension at the same time. Reports from the contingent aboveground were of a similar nature: no opposition.

"We have flung at them every single missile in our possession," commented Borcak, the appointed commander. "But there has been no return fire!"

Ferene took Neshi aside for a few seconds. "It's awfully strange," he said. "As though they are ignoring the diversion."

Could they have become aware of the Jerusalemite strategy and prepared a trap inside Asframore?

"We go no farther for the moment," Neshi said. "We stop here. Tell the others."

"What do you have in mind?" Ferene asked.

"Scouts must go inside. They must find the unit controlling the force field and render it inoperable. We cannot go into Asframore while any of our forces are restrained above if there is even the slightest possibility that the Natasians are planning something knowing that we are here. We could be murdered one by one while our ground units wait impotently!"

The scouts were selected according to Neshi's orders, several from the northern force, the southern, the eastern, and the western. Each would enter Asframore as stealthily as possible, after seeking out any kind of entrance that seemed even remotely feasible. They would report what they found and when they had discovered the power unit for the force field.

Neshi then ordered the aboveground contingent to pull back and wait.

It was not a very long wait.

"Commander Neshi, there is no one here!" That was the report from each of the four infiltrating groups. "All of Asframore that we can see is deserted! We can stand in the middle and look up to the very top, and we encountered no one."

Neshi and Ferene could scarcely believe in the sanity of their soldiers. "Find the power unit!" Neshi ordered.

Several minutes passed until the next report, and then the tone of the scout was uncertain, nervous, his breathing heavy over the remote unit.

"It was . . . discovered, sir . . . a minute or so ago. . . . We laser blasted it into scrap metal. But, sir—"

"Sergeant, what's wrong?"

"Don't come into this place, I—I beg you!"

Then the connection was broken.

Ferene had overheard. "What could they have encountered inside?" he asked, knowing there was no immediate answer but still needing to put forth the question.

"How well do you know this one?" Neshi asked.

"Enough to realize that whatever it was that made him act like that must have been—"

They were interrupted by sounds coming from the remote unit. "No! It's . . . the pain!"

Neshi made an instant decision, summoning Unit Commander Borcak on his remote unit. "Have you any missiles left?" Neshi asked.

"Just three."

"Fire them at the entrance."

"Yes, sir!"

Seconds later, the ground shook with the impact of the missiles hitting Asframore.

"The force field is gone," Borcak confirmed. "The front of Asframore is in rubble."

"Then send your soldiers on in, Unit Commander Borcak."

"It will be done as you say."

Neshi returned his attention to the scouts already inside Asframore, trying to get them to respond.

Nothing.

"Ferene, it is as though they have been swallowed up."

Neshi decided to go inside in full force. The section of tunnels he and his warriors occupied led directly up into the north wing of Asframore; the three other wings would be entered by the groups under other division commanders. They broke through quickly, using their portable laserpacks, the building materials melting under the intense, concentrated blasts.

One long corridor stretched out before them, leading apparently from the northern side of Asframore, where they were, to the opposite side. There were no doors, nothing but flat metallic walls until they reached what they perceived to be the middle.

Elevators.

"Ferene, you take a group up to the top," Neshi said. "I'll go down below."

Ferene motioned him to one side. "Let me suggest," Ferene countered, "that we are becoming too split up before we fully know the layout. We could be picked off one by one in these smaller groups and not have a chance to regroup."

"So we go up to the top together?"

"And down below together, yes."

Neshi nodded.

Floor by floor, they went to the top, stepping out on a kind of balcony around the entire circumference of Asframore.

"The air is so thin here," Ferene commented.

"A plaque," said one of the soldiers. "Look at this plaque."

Neshi and Ferene joined him to read the plaque on the outer wall of Asframore.

"Go to, let us build . . . a tower, whose top may reach unto heaven."

"They truly believe they can do this," Ferene muttered.

"They truly believe that they can *try*," Neshi added. "Look at all this." He indicated with a sweeping gesture the unfinished state of construction there, the wall extending above them obviously not completed. They could not see all the way to the top.

"When are they going to stop?" Ferene asked. "They will never be able to achieve their goal."

"Another one!" the same soldier exclaimed.

Neshi and Ferene read from the second plaque:

"And this they begin to do: and now nothing will be restrained from them, which they have imagined to do."

As they walked around the top, they found others, various bits and pieces of quotations.

"Come, look at this one," Neshi said as he stood before another plaque, the lettering altogether different from the others.

"And we shall place his image on top, in defiance of the Almighty."

"What could that mean?" Ferene asked, scratching his temple. "What is the Almighty? And look! The lettering is quite different, as though it is something apart from the rest."

"Yes, and whose image are they—"

One of the soldiers came running excitedly toward them. "I climbed all the way up. There's a stairway and," he

152

paused to catch his breath, "a statue of some sort. Weird looking. Can I take you there?"

Both Neshi and Ferene nodded and followed the soldier.

The sight of the statue was startling. It must have been fifteen or twenty yards tall. The feet were giant claws, as were the hands. The body was massive, with a long tail at the end. And coming out of the back were wings.

"What in the—" Neshi started to say.

"The face, Neshi. It hasn't been completed," Ferene said, color draining from his own.

There were vague hints of what it would look like: long nose, almost like a beak—

"Down in the lower level! We've found the labs!" the voice came shrilly over Neshi's remote unit.

He could feel a clamminess spread over him. He turned and looked at Ferene.

"You don't have to go," his friend said.

"As commander, I do," he said with a decisiveness that belied his state of mind.

21

They all went down in the elevators, past the floor where they first entered Asframore and several levels beneath that. They entered a very large room filled with cages, long tables, medical apparatus, cabinets, and a number of transparent round cylinders. Even the toughest soldiers blanched at what they saw.

"They're *growing* arms and legs!" one of them shouted.

The cylinders were filled with limbs, some quite small, others normal size. In trays on the tables they found eyes, hearts, and brains. Stacked against one of the walls were the portafreezer units used by the teams sent out to secure limbs. These were crucial in the transport of hearts and brains, particularly the latter, which remained viable for only twenty minutes or less. Cryogenics had been perfected on Neshi's world and enabled the freezing of limbs and tissue for later, but due to the critical time factor,

155

Trans Units had to be ready to move at a moment's notice, equipped with portafreezers and the necessary drugs to hasten an artificially induced period of hibernation.

Spaced evenly in the walls around the main room were entrances to smaller ones. Ferene stood before one of these, looked in, and went on to the next. Then he stumbled back from the fourth doorway.

Neshi had been standing beside one of the tables, looking at the grisly contents of a square tray. He glanced up as his friend approached him.

"Operating rooms," Ferene said.

Neshi saw that he was exceedingly nervous. "What is it?" he asked.

"Perhaps I should say nothing."

Neshi looked at him. "What are you trying to tell me, old friend?"

"Etarina!" Ferene burst out, tears coming to his eyes despite his efforts to stop them.

"You mean that you have found where it happened, where Etarina's body was?"

He had difficulty coping with that possibility. "But how can you be sure, Ferene?"

"Not where her body was, Neshi. Where it *is!*"

For a couple of seconds, what Ferene told him just wouldn't sink in. When it did, Neshi could scarcely control his emotions. "Where, Ferene? Which room?"

"You don't want to see it."

"Ferene, I must."

"Her body, Neshi, Etarina's body is still alive!"

Neshi started to push past.

"You must listen," Ferene pleaded. "I think they've been using her as some sort of primary guinea pig. They transplanted her brain but kept the rest of her sustained somehow."

Neshi almost knocked Ferene over as he made his way to one room, then another.

Etarina!

Covered by a sheet, the body was breathing. A low moan escaped from between those familiar lips. At first the eyes were closed. Her long, beautiful hair had been shaved off; she was completely bald. The top of her head was gone. In the cavity inside, held there by sutures and thin plastic siding, was what must have been someone else's brain in Etarina's body.

Next to that table was another, on it the body of the hunchback, the top of that head also open, but empty.

He walked forward toward the first table.

Suddenly Etarina's eyes opened and looked at him. Her lips parted to say something, and her left hand started to reach upward. "Baba!"

His own mind exploded with shock and revulsion. The Natasians must have put Etarina's brain back into her body in an attempt to discover what went wrong.

He reached out to touch that upraised hand, their fingers meeting.

So cold.

There were wires attached to her wrist. In fact, there were wires all over her body, more than a dozen in the brain alone, leading to machines loaded with gauges and levers and dials and buttons.

Tears were pouring down her cheeks.

He wiped them away with a paper tissue from a pocket in his uniform, but they kept coming.

She couldn't speak anymore, that one precious word having taken all her strength. Abruptly she started coughing, a racking cough that was tearing her up inside. Several of the wires attached to her body were ripped out, and blood began to color the white sheet.

Her left hand moved, pointing to his holstered beam-pistol.

"No, my love, no!" he said.

But then, in an awful burst of clarity, he knew there was no alternative. This was Etarina alive, in one sense, but not actually living, her body attached to wires capable of animating her but not much more than that.

He saw in her eyes a pleading that he could not ignore, could not resist. As he stood back, took the pistol, and aimed it at her, for a fleeting instant there was something else in her eyes, a fading reminder of the love they once knew.

His beloved smiled so very briefly, then her head turned slightly to one side and her eyes closed. She had not required his help, after all.

A cry escaped his lips, a cry with unbearable anguish in it, as though he had experienced the journey of death with her. Shaken, he stumbled to the door.

Ferene was standing in the main room, the other Jerusalemites behind him. A hundred soldiers there, and in the corridor outside, also waiting, several hundred more. Ferene's gaze met his, the two of them communicating as only the closest of friends could, and Neshi realized that it all rested on his shoulders now, more than before. They were in Asframore. They could plunge a thousand daggers into the heart of the Natasians' center of control and power if he could put what had happened at least temporarily into some inner recess of his brain, perhaps later to bring it out again, and face the sorrow, the shock, the awfulness of those moments so that he himself could go on without being an emotional and psychological cripple, but not now because three thousand Jerusalemites in various rooms and corridors of Asframore needed his strength as their strength, his stability and courage to inspire them to confront this most elusive of enemies, to meet the Natasians face-to-face, not knowing, yea, dreading what they would find.

"Commander," one of the soldiers said, "we've heard from the three other units. They've met up in a huge auditoriumlike room roughly in the middle of this place."

"Directions?"

"Yes, sir."

"Let's go."

22

The room was indeed huge, circular in shape but totally barren of appointments of any kind.

"Nothing here!" exclaimed Ferene.

The walls were of an apparently metallic substance, reaching upward two stories or more, and absolutely smooth. Nearly a thousand of the Jerusalemites could fit within the room without being crowded.

Neshi signaled Borcak, who was still outside with his troops.

"We will be most careful, of that you have my guarantee, and my thanks for the warning," he assured Neshi. "We are now starting across the lake."

Neshi's attention focused on a Jerusalemite who was waving at him excitedly.

"Sir, put your face right up to the wall on this side," the soldier told him.

Neshi did precisely that. It was transparent, like one-way glass. On the other side, he could see the base of a sleek-looking ship!

"The Departure Date can be adjusted according to the circumstances."

The words came back to him on thin fingers of apprehension that grabbed the base of his spine and spread chilly tendrils throughout his body.

He took Ferene to one side. "What do you make of this?" he asked.

"I have no idea as yet."

Suddenly, the walls of the room changed. No longer opaque, they became transparent. The several-stories-high ship could be seen clearly—a towering majestic work of engineering.

But then, looking in at *them*, were the Natasians!

The Natasians indeed were not of flesh and blood. They were will-o'-the-wisp spectral shapes, visible, but only barely. They were amorphous, changing one minute into faces without bodies, the next into bodies without faces, visible, then gone, then visible again, like fireflies over the moors at night, and yet infinitely more terrifying—a terror that froze the heart and made the mind scream with fear.

Panic spread through the Jerusalemites.

Neshi stepped forward, trying desperately to calm them, but his words were drowned out by the booming voice that swept them all like a tidal wave:

"VERY BRAVE. VERY NOBLE. THE LEADER OF HIS TROOPS. HOW MUCH TO BE ADMIRED YOU ARE."

A pause, then: *"YOU HAVE BEEN WONDERING ABOUT THE MEANING OF THE TERM DEPARTURE DATE. YOU WILL SOON FIND OUT."*

Laughter filled the room—hysterical, shrieking laughter. The shapes on the other side of the wall became more and more excited.

Suddenly there was no wall at all, and the shapes were upon them. They entered some bodies and destroyed them from within, leaving only shrunken husks like rotten fruit that fell in on itself. The odors that were released were rancid, like flesh that had been putrefying under a hot sun. Other Jerusalemites were played with for a bit, chased, allowed to stand, then caused to collapse screaming.

"We can't fight these things! Even my fists go right through them like air!" One of the Jerusalemites came running toward him, a vaporous thing roughly in the shape of a giant spiderlike creature on his back, entering his pores and sucking the life from him, the comrade falling a foot or so from him.

Then Neshi saw Ferene battling a fellow Jerusalemite! He ran over and separated the two of them.

"He's under their control now!" Ferene shouted. "Watch out!"

The Jerusalemite, a mad, slobbering expression on his face, lunged for Neshi.

Neshi had retrieved a knife from his outfit, and the other didn't see this in time. The blade went straight into his heart. He fell down Neshi's front onto the floor. Before he died seconds later, he spoke just six words: "Please, I beg you, forgive me."

Neshi turned to Ferene, who could now hardly stand, his face bruised and bloody, his arm hanging loosely by his side. *"Go!"* Ferene demanded.

"No! I can't desert you," Neshi replied.

"Dying with us is not victory. Go!"

"I will not! Running is cowardice. We can never defeat

these monsters without courage. Only then can we hope for salvation."

Suddenly Asframore shook as though a beast was venting its enormous rage.

"IT IS ODD THAT YOU ARE THE ONE TO USE THAT WORD. YOU WHO WERE DAMNED FROM THE BEGINNING OF YOUR MISERABLE LIFE. BEHOLD, THE MAESTRO OF HELL COMES FORTH TO CLAIM YOU FOREVER!"

Abruptly everything in the room was frozen like a videodisc scene set in still mode. From the opposite end of the room, in the area where the wall had been, a creature three times his height lumbered toward Neshi. Its feet were cloven hooves, its hands like talons, its face lined with boils, the flesh green and yellow.

"YOU BOTH ARE MINE. MY NATURE IS WITHIN YOU. COME TO ME, AND WE DANCE TOGETHER OVER THE BODIES OF THE VANQUISHED."

"What you say are lies!" Neshi screamed. "You are a loathsome monster spewing forth corruption!"

Neshi held Ferene as firmly and gently as he could, inching backward, away from the creature. He was only a few yards from a ladder leading up into the ship, then only a few feet. As they climbed up its rungs, Neshi turned for an instant and saw something he would remember for the rest of his life.

The creature had turned and approached one of the bodies. It was bending over the limp flesh, absorbing it molecule by molecule, until there was nothing left. Bigger because of its meal, it went to other bodies and assimilated them as well, though some were yet alive and their dying cries rent the air. The creature continued growing, the other bodies disappearing into its own, and still it went on, the Jerusalemites helpless, unable to do anything but cry as the most awful pain rent their consciousness before they became a part of the creature.

Just as the door to the ship was closing, the creature turned toward Neshi, and there was a smile of sorts on its face, if something so perverse and unholy could be thought capable of smiling.

"WE'VE WON, YOU KNOW. THIS INDEED IS DEPARTURE DATE. NOT OURS, BUT YOURS, TECH DETECTIVE NESHI. YOU THOUGHT WE WERE THE ONES PLANNING TO LEAVE. OH, EVENTUALLY, YES, AND THEN ON TO ANOTHER WORLD, FOLLOWED BY ANOTHER, CONTINUING THE WAR IN HEAVENLY PLACES.

"BUT WE ARE FRANKLY HAVING TOO MUCH FUN HERE, NOW! WE WANTED YOU OUT OF THE WAY. YOUR SENSE OF DECENCY WAS GETTING TO BE A PROBLEM. WITH YOU GONE, THERE IS NO BARRIER TO WHATEVER DELICIOUS GAMES WE WANT TO PLAY."

Neshi tried to stop the door from shutting but couldn't. Mocking laughter greeted his effort.

"WE COULD HAVE KILLED YOU AT ANY GIVEN MOMENT. BUT IT IS FAR MORE FORBIDDING FOR OTHERS TEMPTED TO FOLLOW IN YOUR FOOTSTEPS TO KNOW THAT YOUR FATE IS NOT THE MERCIFUL ONE OF SUDDEN DEATH BUT RATHER THE CONTINUING MISERY THAT YOU INDEED WILL FACE FOR THE REST OF YOUR NORMAL LIFE.

"YOU HAVE ENOUGH FUEL TO TAKE YOU UNTIL THE END OF YOUR DAYS. WE HAVE MADE VERY SURE OF THAT. YOUR SHIP IS VERY EFFICIENT IN THAT REGARD. PERHAPS YOUR FOOD MAY RUN OUT MUCH

SOONER, IF YOU ARE NOT ABLE TO EAT OF THE HAR- VEST OF ANY OF THE UNKNOWN WORLDS YOU WILL UNDOUBTEDLY VISIT."

Very loud evil laughter then, shaking his very being. At last the creature stopped, adding only a few final words: *"FAREWELL, TECH DETECTIVE NESHI, AS YOU NOW BEGIN TO WANDER TILL THE END OF YOUR DAYS IN THE COLD, EMPTY DARKNESS OF THE UNIVERSE."*

The door was shut, cutting off everything else. Apparently on some kind of autopilot mechanism, the ship was already beginning the launch process. He could see, for an instant, the terrified faces of those he was leaving behind.

In a very short while, after Neshi and Ferene had strapped themselves into the two seats in front of the complicated-looking control panel, the ship had broken through the planet's stratosphere.

Part Two

Behind the dim unknown,
Standeth God within the shadow,
keeping watch above his own.
JAMES RUSSELL LOWELL

23

The shock of leaving their world literally flattened them against the backs of their seats, their facial muscles stretching in a dozen different directions as though made of rubber and not nerve-lined flesh that rebelled from the unaccustomed torture.

Neshi felt raw, chilling panic as he and Ferene were thrust into space with no clue as to what would happen next.

After countless centuries of colonization and technologization, there had been remarkable advances in science, medicine, and virtually every area of life, but it seemed that the race's long-held desire to go back into space would never be realized. No one was sure why; the deficiency of achievement in this one area was never explained by government officials. The questions just ceased because they did not have direct impact upon anyone's everyday life.

And yet there they were, in a ship constructed in such secrecy that only the vaguest of clues about it had leaked out. There had been the scattered hint, gossip centering around "something mysterious the government's got going," "a diversion of funds for a hush-hush construction project," but nothing more concrete than whispers between friends.

At first there was nothing either of them could say or do but watch through the forward portals, speechless, more than a little uncomprehending, half expecting something to suggest that they had been thrown together in a common dream and eventually reality would snap its fingers and awaken them.

But that was not to be the case. Even if he could properly operate the ship, there was no other destination of which he was aware.

Somehow he would have to get accustomed to a rather aimless wandering through space, perhaps one day accidentally stumbling upon another planet on which he could land and start over, if the supplies held out long enough. But there was no assurance of that or anything else, and in fact he could no longer even measure time, and the loss of that measuring stick added to his pervasive sense of isolation.

He stood in the middle of the small control compartment, looking at the instruments directly in front of him— row after row of dials and switches and levers— bewildering in their number and yet not totally unknown to him once he recalled seeing them during his Tech Detective training.

Leaning back on the second seat facing the panel, Ferene was moaning slightly, his eyes closed, his mouth slightly open. Other than that, there was no noise, the sounds of the engines being well muffled at the opposite end of the ship.

No one else for millions of miles, Neshi thought.

He walked a couple of feet to one of the four portals in the cramped quarters. He had never before been afraid of heights but, for that instant, nearly alone in the vastness that stretched on in every direction, he felt as though he were on the top floor of a very tall building, looking over the edge, and suddenly the building evaporated from under him, and he was suspended there, waiting to fall. Yet in this case it seemed that he could fall forever and never land.

When that sensation passed, another swept in to take its place, that of being in a kind of fancy coffin, its sides tightly packed around him. He wanted desperately to get out, but there was no possibility of that, and the coffin seemed to be getting smaller.

He realized, with considerable surprise, that he was trembling.

Apparently the ship was equipped with instruments for gathering information on the oxygen content and other important details of worlds to be glimpsed in the travels ahead, in case there were any upon which a landing could be attempted. But even so, it was literally a guessing game with so many worlds from which to choose. One wrong choice, one misreading of the instruments out of rank inexperience, and he might land on the wrong kind of world and not be able to retreat from it, facing life-forms he didn't want to begin to imagine.

The ship, which seemed so immense in its cradle, was actually much smaller inside—surprisingly so. And that wasn't all that surprised Neshi and Ferene. The ship was fully stocked with food and supplies, which was indication that every step he had taken, every move he had made, had been anticipated and he was heading in precisely the direction they had planned for him.

How much foresight the Natasians had had. How advanced their planning was.

. . . how long ago and where?

That question rose like the unanswerable enigma it was, tantalizing in its tattered threads, none of which, he suspected, could ever be connected, and yet begging to be neatly wrapped up and fully answered, the purpose of all that had happened so clear that he would feel stupid for not guessing it sooner.

There was even a supply of medicine and bandages that Neshi used to bind up his friend's wounds.

But Ferene grew worse. His wounds became infected and he rambled, talking about the early years of their friendship, how envious he was when Neshi found a mate, how sad when she was killed.

"After that, you wanted to track down any criminal you were assigned, to make sure he would cause no more misery to anyone else. You even actively, some might say, zealously, solicited assignments after doing research about a particular act of violence that had been reported, especially if there were parallels to your own tragedy. It was your continuing way of avenging her death."

Etarina, Neshi spoke without words. *Etarina, if only it could have been otherwise, my dear one.*

When he wasn't by Ferene's side giving him liquids, holding him gently, talking to him in reassuring tones, Neshi wandered about the ship.

It had basically five sections: the navigational section at

the front; sleeping quarters next; the area where food and other supplies were stored; the knowledge section; and the engine/power compartment.

All of these except the last were little more than cramped cubicles. While the knowledge section was the worst in terms of space limitations, Neshi was grateful that it was even there. The library of videodiscs was not Hall of Knowledge size in scope, of course, but more comprehensive than might have been expected under the circumstances.

He would eventually go through every disc, even those that were of marginal interest, breaking the sameness of life for the moment, until there were no fresh tapes left and he was reduced to rerunning the same ones again and again.

At the start he was drawn to the discs for information about stars and planets, not expecting much help from his non-space-traveling race. He found much more than he had anticipated. There were names and diameters and atmospheric densities, and much more, everything neatly cataloged in startling detail. Planet after planet, solar system after solar system:

"**Nowsnatas**: A planet colonized after yet another Armageddon (*see* Disc 316) but to no avail, all our careful work over the centuries finally destroyed by Havohej's emissaries, who forced us off its surface to continue the battle elsewhere."

This was followed by a detailed listing of the animal life, plant life, number of bodies of water, and more, ending with one word: "**Terminated.**"

An entire world destroyed, perhaps nothing left of the civilization.

Who were the emissaries mentioned? He searched for Disc 316 and slipped it into the little slot under the view-screen in front of him.

"**Armageddon:** Access denied."

The previous entry referred to another that had been overridden. He tried twice more but got the same response.

A single control key allowed him to transfer the coordinates for Nowsnatas to the navigational equipment in the nose of the ship. He found himself hurrying back to the panel to see what the new information revealed about the proximity of Nowsnatas.

Ferene was lying on the floor in a pool of blood.

Neshi rushed to his side.

"Dear friend, please forgive me," Neshi said, deep concern and regret mixed in his voice.

Ferene was barely conscious. "I am dying. Nothing can prevent that now."

His body shook as pain rippled through it. "I want to be returned to the space from which we all came."

The idea froze Neshi's mind.

"I can almost see your thoughts, my dear, dear Neshi. You think you will be more alone than ever before in your life. It is bad enough now, even with me here. But that is why my body cannot remain in this ship. There is no way to keep me—"

He started sobbing. "Neshi, hold me now, will you? I feel as though I am already out there, drifting, and yet alive, past a thousand worlds, nay, ten thousand strange and unknown ones, and having no home on any until one day there is nothing left of me, even my body gone, its bits and pieces scattered across the heavens."

Neshi held his friend tightly, blood seeping onto himself. He could feel Ferene's strength dissipating rapidly now.

"Neshi. Neshi, I feel your arms but I cannot see you. So cold now. I see instead a creature with a long mane—"

Suddenly Ferene's eyes opened wide and clear. He reached up his left hand to wipe the tears from Neshi's face, stopping in midair, his body trembling once, and then the hand dropped back to the floor.

Neshi held Ferene's form for what must have been a long time. He could not possibly have guessed the number of minutes or hours. He only knew that he did not want to let go, that he had to resist as long as he could granting Ferene's wish, putting him into a plastic bag or whatever else he could find and then dragging him to the air lock and leaving him as he went back to the control panel, sat down, and pulled the lever that would open the hatch.

. . . *past a thousand worlds, nay, ten thousand strange and unknown ones.*

Finally he watched with fragments of memories across the synapses of his brain as his friend's body was being sucked out into the transcendent darkness.

24

For quite a while after Ferene was gone, Neshi found himself speaking out by reflex and asking his friend a question, then catching himself. The tears would always flow after that, tears that six months before he would not have thought himself capable of, his reservoir long dried-up because of the way Etarina had been taken from him.

He also dreamed of sad and wonderful memories and then, in the midst of it all, something that wasn't merely recalled from the past but seemed quite new and devastating.

The planet of his birth was suddenly engulfed in flame before his eyes, flame that spread a reddish cloud around most of its surface.

He thought he saw, as its bits and pieces exploded outward in a million directions, in the midst of the swirling destruction, a hideous face laughing. And then the expression changed, the mocking laughter suddenly gone, a look of fear apparent, the flames swirling around it instead of below, consuming it, sending screams of pain echoing through time and space.

Gone.

The planet, the mass of fire, and the face were gone, and replacing all that—indeed eliminating it—he glimpsed a different place, a place upon the streets of which walked another race, like his own, and yet not, smiling, a sense of joy radiating from them and around them.

Those streets were bright, like gold. And in the distance, he glimpsed a throne surrounded by light so pure, so radiant.

A powerful voice came then, unclearly reaching his ears. He hungered for the words, his very being somehow eager for every syllable. He reached out, started to speak, wanting to respond, however blindly.

A hand on his shoulder, cold, hard, like a claw, and he turned away.

Neshi awoke shivering, wanting someone to talk to, someone who could take the strangeness of that dream and peel it apart, layer by layer, so it was not a mystery but something so thoroughly dissected and explained and understood that it would never terrorize him again.

Was it a premonition of some sort? A warning? The vision stayed with him, constantly poking up through his consciousness.

If in fact his world, his home, one day would be blown apart, to exist only as largely unconnected molecules of matter tumbling invisibly in space, then who or what would be responsible? Surely not the Natasians, because they would not subjugate a world only to destroy it. But if not those evil ones, then who?

It struck him as particularly sad that he had no photographs of Etarina or Ferene or anyone else with whom he had been close over the years, all of them left behind on a world that might become mere nothingness. *Everything returns to dust or a form of it,* he mused. *Etarina's ashes, our home, all broken down into the tiniest of particles, nothing more than a few memories. Then perhaps these also will disappear as hunger weakens me and saps my mind as well as my body.*

There was nothing he could do; he had no choices at that point other than suicide. He could take his life, or he could stay alive and alert for as long as possible, hoping to stumble upon some planet that would give him a new lease on life.

"I will not give up!" he declared to the empty sleeping compartment. But as the supplies dwindled and the grating monotony grew oppressive, he wondered how much the circumstances would undermine his determination.

Ultimately he had little or no choice but to return to one of the hibernation chambers as often as possible. These were located in the sleeping quarters and looked like displaced sleeptime cylinders. At first he was quite nervous about setting the timer and getting inside, but he realized that the control center for all the cylinders had blown up along with everything else back home.

What hibernation gave him was a temporary cessation of all but minimal brain waves, heartbeat, and other bodily functions necessary to sustain life. In this manner, the passage of years was reduced to mere days or weeks as far as wear and tear on his body was concerned. The cylinder could be timed: at the end of each cycle he was awakened and brought completely out of hibernation. According to a calendar, it might have been just two weeks of *his* time, but judging by the universes around him in all directions, a century might have passed.

There were three hibernation chambers on the ship. *Why three?* he wondered. *If they planned everything so carefully, why three and not just one?*

If it had not been for the discs, Neshi might have been driven to the edge of insanity. Even so, there were times when he thought of stepping into the air lock and allowing himself to be sucked out into space. There would be crushing pain for a few seconds and then oblivion. Despite the momentary temptations, he would always return to the discs and find something intriguing among them, taking each out of its receptacle with such abiding anticipation that sometimes his hand shook.

When he came to the *W*s, he happened upon one of the most tantalizing discoveries of all: **"The Wanderer."**

He had not seen that reference before, either in the ship or during his informational forays into the Hall of Knowledge.

"Access denied."

Not again!

But why? Why mention The Wanderer or Armageddon and deny entry to the information stored about them?

Neshi started pacing the corridor outside the library compartment. Both entries were obviously of some significance. How could he break through? Once seated back in the library, he tried several combinations of code. Nothing. He stayed with it for what must have been hours at a stretch. Every so often he would push himself away from the disc unit and leave the library to get some food, then come back to try again and again.

Some words came through in scattered scraps, which was not surprising in view of the way he was hacking into the storage banks.

"But we are not defeated though Nowsnatas is in ruins. There are other worlds beyond numbering. We move from one to another. There is no reason we must face the Lake of . . . it is all a lie. Triumphant, we will push on to the gates. . . .

He tried to read on, but no more fragments could be coaxed out of the disc. He pressed one key, got a printout of the information that had been gained, and took this back to the navigation compartment. He sat down and studied it.

Who was moving from one planet to another, leaving desolation in their wake? His eyes abruptly focused on the word *Nowsnatas*, shifting to the last five letters and mentally adding four more: *Natas . . . ians!*

The same root letters in both!

Perspiration broke out on the palms of his large hands. *The Departure Date.*

That phrase from the plastic fragment Ferene had given him came to his mind.

"We move from one to another."

And finally, "Triumphant, we will push on to the gates."

"Nowsnatas is in ruins. The Departure Date can be adjusted according to the circumstances. We move from one to another. Triumphant, we will push on to the gates."

He spoke those words aloud, stringing together sections as coherently as he could.

The Natasians had been to other planets, had left them

ruined and useless, and now his world was another casualty. But if his dream somehow proved a prophecy, there would not be even a pile of rock to show that it ever existed.

Just what would happen back there if the planet did not in fact explode? He had learned enough about their decadence before going to Asframore to make him shudder. Without much of a threat from the few remaining Jerusalemites, the Natasians could institute all manner of corruption, such a wave of it that the games in The Dome would have seemed the work of innocent children in comparison.

The emissaries mentioned previously—had they interceded once again, driven the Natasians off his world, then turned it into fragments throughout the galaxy?

He was tired, his mind unwilling to continue trying to fathom such mysteries. For a split second before he drifted off to sleep, too drained to walk the short distance to the sleeping compartment, he thought he saw Ferene's body floating by the portal in front of him. Yet he knew that this could not be, that he would have to be prepared for other hallucinations ahead in the uncertain journey that remained—phantoms born of weariness and numbing sameness and perhaps a fleeting moment of hope—phantoms so fragile and senseless they soon became a mocking face, laughing directly into his own.

25

Eventually, he knew, he would no longer be content with the aimless journey to which it was so easy to submit, surrounded by a protective metallic cocoon, no demands made on him, until one day he would simply close his eyes and be embraced by an even more compelling nothingness.

The part of his nature that guaranteed his rebellion against the Natasians also ensured his growing impatience with this wandering, the potential of the circumstances reaching a self-proscribed inevitability that tore at his nerve ends and made him pace impatiently up and down the ship.

Some planet, he thought. *Any planet!*

There was no paucity of choices; innumerable worlds were ready for his exploration.

His first landing was a sorry affair. It was one thing to sit back while the ship was on autopilot but quite another to take over its operation and navigate through a meteorite-littered path to land on an unknown planet.

At one point he nearly gave up, forsaking any adventuresome side trips. But he kept on, broke through a planet's upper atmosphere, and saw a place teeming with life. Yet it was twisted life, life that squirmed in grotesque slitherings, creatures of well-nigh indescribable repulsiveness, fighting one another, killing and devouring.

He turned the ship away and left, hurtling back into space. Some while later, as he looked back to where he had been, he saw a burst of brightness, red and orange and yellow, then only tiny shards that glowed briefly and were gone.

Was that the fate of my world? he asked himself. *The conclusion of a million years of history?*

Perhaps the answer would remain as indiscernible as what the future would bring him, or any purpose in its midst.

Eventually he came upon Nowsnatas. There were ruins on the planet, remainders of buildings countless centuries old. He found thousands of grave markers in a single field, and scratched in wood were just three words: THE LAST BATTLE.

He came upon ancient machines eaten through by rust, clogging the streets of a once-great city. In one building, he saw what must have been the collective knowledge of that civilization. On the floor were scraps of books and videodiscs, virtually all destroyed by the passage of time.

On one split sheet of plastic, there were only two numbers: " . . . lation 20:15." On another he found just a single word, partially obliterated: " . . . mnation."

But then he came upon the drawing. The image depicted was familiar to him.

And in the distance, on a throne, surrounded by light so pure, so radiant . . .

Around that throne were winged beings of such majesty that Neshi was driven to tears at the sight of them. And on the throne was a face obscured by a coating of what could have been dried blood. He could perceive only a hint of what it looked like, but even so, he knew he gazed upon a face quite unlike any he had seen before, a face he wished he could see fully, a face he could never describe but also never forget.

He put the plastic-backed drawing back where he had found it, though he would regret doing that during the time to follow, during the long, long journey.

Later, in the very center of that city, he stood before the ruins of a very large building, only the foundation surviving, and in the midst of the rubble, a statue. The feet of the figure were more like giant claws, as were the hands. The body was massive, with a long tail at the end. And coming out of the back were . . .

The similarity was striking, and like the statue on his home planet, this, too, had been destroyed, mocking whatever it was supposed to commemorate.

Though he had found no life, he could not escape the sensation of being watched. That feeling would be duplicated on other planets he visited, dozens of them, each as dead as the one preceding and the one following, the tombs of races now gone, their achievements unknown to the rest of the universe.

But on Nowsnatas there was a special hopelessness that mocked the dead dreams. He stood there, surrounded by the shattered residue of an ancient time. That sense of utter despair—of lostness—magnified itself, sweeping over him in suffocating wave after wave.

He felt a sudden compulsion to run, to run as fast as he could back to the ship and leave that place. And yet, grabbing hold of him was the special fear that, as previously, all the others would be little different.

He spun around and around.

This is all there is, will ever be.

The voice was inside him.

We fight on, truly we do. We gain a victory here, a victory there, but in the end—

He screamed at the terrible images assaulting him, of living shapes aflame, faces twisted with agony.

And in the air, a distant sound, closer, like the beating of a thousand, nay, ten thousand wings. . . .

Louder and louder, until it was deafening, until he had to close his eyes and clamp his hands over his ears, trying to block it out.

Gone.

He opened his eyes.

At first there was nothing. Then he heard a sound behind him and spun around. Sitting on a piece of that broken statue he saw a single white bird, its wings dripping blood.

Life!

He walked toward it, reaching out his hand. The bird fluttered its wings but remained. And then he sat down in front of it.

"Where have you come from?" he asked. "Are you the only one left?"

With that the bird took wing and flew off toward one of

the taller buildings—or rather shells of buildings—in that city. It went inside. He followed it.

Countless numbers of the white birds sat on fallen pieces of the building, nestled together on the skeletal frame, or just flying around. One of them landed on his head, another on his shoulder.

So much life!

He started crying. He had begun to think the entire length and breadth of everything that was had died and he was the only living being left, jumping from tomb to tomb in a ship that would eventually become his own.

He closed his eyes, overcome with the ecstasy of that moment, thinking if only he could plant seeds and watch fruits and vegetables grow. . . .

Something started digging into his shoulder and the top of his head.

He opened his eyes.

The birds were gone. On his shoulder stood a grotesque miniaturized version of the image on that statue atop As-framore, alive, grinning at him, and digging its claws into his flesh.

Ten thousand of them swept into that building, their faces asnarl.

He grabbed the creature on his shoulder and the one on his head and tossed them to one side, then ran outside.

That same white bird was sitting in the same spot on the fallen statue. It looked at him as he hesitated a moment, and then it seemed to shake its head just before it took flight.

He continued running until he almost passed out, back to the ship and quickly inside, and in a short while he had blasted off from Nowsnatas.

26

Neshi sat at the control panel after the ship had left the planet. His hands were shaking. He knew the only way he could escape madness was to push what he had seen and heard deep within his subconscious, with the hope that it all would remain buried there and forgotten, as though none of it had ever happened.

He tried very hard to control the shaking. After a while, he succeeded, only to have it start up again, not violently, just a slight trembling, really, his nerves twisted so badly for so long that it was a miracle he had not collapsed altogether.

Neshi pushed himself away from the control panel and stalked out of the navigational quarters, heading down the corridor to the room where all the supplies were stored. Groping through several boxes, he found what he wanted: liquid medicine that would calm him.

It helped for a little while, and then he had to take more. And before long, having consumed too much, he threw up all over the floor. Then, in pain and dizziness, he sank down in the midst of the slop and passed out.

Finally he managed to get through the trauma of Now-snatas. There were frequent moments of regression, but what helped was a far more basic fact of life: his supplies were dwindling. He had to find another world, a more hospitable one from which he could gain edible substances to replenish his stock. The tyranny of the past gave way to the survival considerations of the present.

He touched down on one planet after another. None were alive. All gave evidence of tumultuous demise. What had once been buildings were now shattered ruins, rusty carcasses of machines, craters plunging deep below the surface, bubbling beds of red-hot molten rock sending thick geysers of smoke into the air—or else cold blackness, even the forces of destruction dead.

All were the same, each successive scene a replay of the one before it, a tapestry of violent destruction, tombs of extinct races spinning in their orbits, dead and forgotten.

Eventually he passed a world covered by swirling clouds, the heat so intense that he knew he could not land on it and survive. Another had a spinning band of galactic refuse around it.

So it went, on and on. The food ran down to a few crumbs. Dizzy spells were afflicting him with increasing frequency.

His hunger more strident now, he was becoming progressively weaker. . . .

Etarina, if I could just hear you whisper to me, hear you say that everything will be fine.

He looked out into the blackness. Directly ahead was another planet covered by mistiness. He was tempted to pass it by. It, too, would surely prove to be a husk, like all the others.

Several of the instruments on the panel before him began to oscillate wildly. A vibration started within the ship. The temperature changed, going upward in jumps of several degrees each.

Suddenly the ship lurched with great violence. Immediately, he lost power. The gauges started going dead one after the other. Only the auxiliary boosters remained partially operational.

He knew he had to mitigate the impact of hitting the surface of the planet and cut the boosters to fractional power.

He could see details now: mountains and a wide stretch of barrenness akin to what he had witnessed elsewhere. Nearby a blanket of steam arose from a small body of water.

There was water here! Could there be life? For a brief instant, he saw figures looking up in shock just before metal met rock and sand and his mind exploded in a burst of blood-red color.

Part Three

Truth is a flower in whose neighbourhood others must wither.

E.M. FORSTER

27

When Neshi regained consciousness, he was resting on a soft bed of woollike cushioning. Overhead he glimpsed a wood-framed roof thatched of hay and branches that had baked together into a hard substance.

The air was dry, hot.

I am unable to move! Have I become paralyzed?

He heard movement, glanced slightly to his left.

A creature of near-pure whiteness, fragile looking.

A smile crossed that extraordinary face, a face with translucent skin, its veins and some of its internal organs quite visible.

"You were close to death." The words came from between very thin lips.

Just one more drop in the Currents of the Cosmos! Etarina was there, but he would never know her again, never see her face as close as this strange one directly above him. Her spirit was lost, nameless and shapeless.

"You were talking in your distress about someone." Words came again, a look of concern on that strange face.

I can never forget you, my love. Not even when I am close to death and pain overtakes me.

"You were bidding her good-bye. You were talking of seeing her in your mind one last moment."

Tears came to Neshi's eyes.

"Tears cleanse," the voice said. "Go ahead."

And cry he did, relentlessly, despite pain from the injuries caused by the crash.

Finally he asked about his ship.

"It is quite intact," the being assured him.

"Intact? How could that be?"

"You landed on a cushion of soft moss with dirt underneath. There was no better spot."

Then she told him something else that was even more astounding. "You are the second one who has stumbled upon us."

"The second? There has been another before me?"

"Someone else once came to our planet."

"Is he still here?"

"No. He died a very long time ago."

He could detect that she wasn't telling him all the details. "There's more, isn't there?" he probed.

"Get well first. With health, with strength, will come what you seek."

He fell asleep a few moments later, reliving in a dream portions of his odyssey through space, then the landing. In this vision he saw another ship, saw a name on the side but couldn't make out the letters.

When he awoke, the same female was there; he wondered if she had ever left.

"You are different from anyone we have ever seen," came that gentle, soothing voice. "You are quite big and solid and have so much hair!"

He had to admit to himself that the contrast between them was striking. He felt quite huge in comparison. He blinked several times, clearing the last fogginess from his vision. To his left were two more of the beings, both the same: tall, thin, translucent skin, large eyes, and tiny ears like needle holes.

His nose wiggled as he noticed something else: a sweet odor. "What is that?" he spoke at last.

"We make perfume here," the one apparently tending to him replied proudly.

"Perfume?"

"Many kinds. We sell it to traders who journey here from other parts of our world."

He tried to sit up but was still very weak. "Your world?" he asked. "What world is that?"

"It is called Nede."

"Strange name."

"To us, no."

He smiled at that, realizing how silly it was to say what he did.

"Very sorry," he offered.

"Accepted."

"What is your name?"

"Graita."

"A beautiful name."

"Thank you."

"Are you—"

"Female?"

"Yes! How did you—"

"We do not read minds, but we *are* very intuitive."

She stood, a movement so simple yet so filled with gracefulness.

"You seem almost to be dancing," he remarked.

"We dance with the joy of life. We dance with nearness to our Creator."

He was about to ask her what she meant, but she and the two others were gone in an instant.

He lay back, closing his eyes, trying to absorb what was happening.

He came back to consciousness and drifted out of it innumerable times, but Graita and others were with him constantly. When some new pain ripped through his body, one of them would bathe his forehead and whisper softly to him.

And they would sing songs of peace, songs of comfort and hope, songs of healing melody and tenderness.

When memories of Etarina would come back to him, Graita would hold his hand and hum. She would reach over and wipe the tears from his cheeks and lie next to him, the touch of her skin like gossamer.

Finally, strength returned. He managed to put Etarina in some back corner of his mind, though he did so with great reluctance and a feeling of betrayal. It was as if he were burying her forever, realizing that she was dead and he was alive, and unless he wanted life to end immediately, he would have to go on. He would have to take the small white hand being offered to him and get up and embrace these kind, loving creatures.

Graita introduced him to a male friend named Dwaun. "We will be in union soon," she told Neshi. She was obviously delighted.

They guided him through the settlement in which the two of them lived. There was a residential section and a commercial section, but except for signs in front of the huts, there was little to distinguish the two.

The air was clear, and they had virtually no crime. "To disobey the laws is to bring shame and grief to all of us."

Neshi saw how close Graita and Dwaun were, how loving they acted toward each other, though she took great pains to point out that they would not be together sexually until the official ceremony of union.

"We have many rules," Dwaun remarked. "Our society is built on them. Our society is controlled by them."

"Why is this so?" Neshi asked.

"It is the only way we can be accepted by the Creator."

"The only way to what?"

"To earn the right of being in His presence one day."

Neshi was astounded by that concept.

Everything he had learned of such matters during his lifetime contradicted the existence of any sense of personality after death. How could these obviously intelligent beings accept so absurd a notion as Someone out there in the cosmos?

They were standing in the settlement's hub, a huge circle large enough for many of the thousand or so citizens to gather. Partway around the circle, in a 180-degree grouping, were governmental huts larger than those in the residential area.

"Our officials follow the same rules as the rest of us," Dwaun commented, unaware of his visitor's skepticism. "Everything is geared toward pleasing Him."

"But how can you believe He exists?"

Dwaun stepped back a bit and looked at him in amazement. "What was it like where you came from?"

Neshi told him. Dwaun was dumbfounded. "Such an evil place!" he exclaimed. "We are not at all like that. Not at all."

It was readily apparent that Dwaun was not merely boastful. Everything did seem the opposite of life on the planet where Neshi had been born and raised.

He saw a seemingly primitive community, not the highly advanced one in which he had grown up, beings who believed in intellectual training but were enslaved to nonsensical beliefs about spirituality.

Neshi noted this as they stood at the rear of a large hut and witnessed an education class in session.

"You can reason with intelligence, I see, about everything except this notion of a Creator," Neshi said.

Every student in the classroom turned around, as did the teacher in front.

One female stood and walked up to him. She introduced herself as Tuati. "You are intelligent yourself," she said. "Why don't you believe?"

"Because it is so ridiculous. We have what we have, what we can see, what we can hear and touch."

"What our senses tell us. Is that it?"

"Yes, you are correct."

He was captivated by this female. Being educated in this society wasn't something that stopped at a certain age. Adult males and females continued their education for many years, and this was one such class.

"What about the sense that tells us God does exist?" she asked.

"God?"

"Yes. That is one of the names we call Him."

"What do you call yourselves?"

"We were once Jerusalemites. Now we are otherwise."

Jerusalemites! He had not heard that name spoken for a very long time. "How do you come by that name?" he inquired.

"It is from God Himself," she said simply.

"You said you were *once* Jerusalemites?" he went on, trying not to show the shock that pervaded every inch of his body.

"We were once unredeemed. We had a sense of what divine reality was, but our minds were darkened. Now we have an opportunity to earn our salvation."

"What gave that to you—that opportunity?" Neshi asked.

"A prophet named J'Sopah Smythe. Brother Smythe received a vision from the Almighty God Himself. We call ourselves Smythians."

Dwaun stepped in then. "You are tiring our guest," he said. "Neshi comes from a place where there was no God, no prophet, no faith."

Immediately a sigh arose from those gathered behind Tuati, as well as Tuati herself. "Was?" she asked. "Why do you say *was*?"

"It is gone," Neshi told her. "At least that is what I dreamed. Judging by what I have seen elsewhere, it may be just what happened." He threw his hands outward in a gesture to indicate an explosion. "Or worse," he added.

"What could be worse?" she asked.

"To be a skeleton in an orbit, exhibiting to the universe your powdering bones."

Tuati bowed her head slightly. "Sad," she said. "Very sad." And then she looked up, that beautiful skin so clear, so pure in appearance. Her cheeks were wet. "I will pray for you," she said with great earnestness.

There was a murmur behind her.

"We all will pray for you," she added, blushing a bit, the effect quite astonishing as her entire face went from pearl white to deep red.

"Thank you," Neshi said with little conviction, fighting a feeling of offense that she thought he needed any prayer to a Creator who simply didn't exist.

28

Much time passed.

An attraction developed between Neshi and Tuati. Perhaps not coincidentally, she was appointed as his personal guide.

He learned much about Nedian society. It was agriculturally based. Nedians raised all their own food through livestock herds or catching marine life out of the plenteous bodies of water on the planet. They built their homes out of the natural materials found everywhere.

And they worshiped a Creator who insisted upon what Neshi grew to feel was a suffocating load of rules and regulations.

"A rule for every act, no matter how simple?" Neshi would say to Tuati as they sat by an azure lake.

"Oh, yes. How else could we know Him?" she would respond.

He was at a loss as to how to answer her. He believed in no divine force or God or Creator in any form. How could he dispute this lovely female's views without being cast in the role of one who would destroy her faith?

"Tuati," he said hesitantly, "on my world there were awful monsters we called the Natasians." And he told her as much as he could about the hated ones.

"They sound evil," she remarked.

"That they are. Or were."

"Let me ask you this: If there was evil on your world, can you say that there was *nothing* in opposition, that there was no good there or elsewhere in the universe?"

"I believe in good—the good of noble thoughts and actions, sacrifices on the part of a few for the survival of many. That is the kind of good I find believable."

"But not the good represented by our God?"

He shook his head sadly.

"You call your evil ones Natasians?"

"Yes."

She was writing in the dirt in front of her with a finger: *Natasians.* She wiped out the last four letters.

"What are you doing?" he asked.

"We have an evil one in whom we believe. We do not place faith in him, but we believe in his existence."

Natas.

"We had the same word on my home planet," Neshi told her.

Tuati didn't seem at all surprised.

"We believe that there is a universal language throughout all of creation."

"And this word seems familiar?" he asked, his attention suddenly riveted.

"Not that way. But *this* way, yes!"

Satan.

"Who is Satan?" he asked.

"The Devil, God's adversary. We can keep him at bay—"

"Through piles of rules, endless heaps of commandments."

"That is what God has told us through J'Sopah Smythe."

"How did he get all this from God?"

"Through a vision."

Neshi spoke logically, compelled to do so by a lifetime in a rationalistic society, but he regretted what he told Tuati as soon as the words left his lips. "Why couldn't that vision have been from Satan? To misdirect you?"

"But it directed us toward God."

"How can you be sure? Have you heard God's response?"

"We have what J'Sopah Smythe has told us."

"Are you perfect as a race?"

"No, we aren't!" she declared, though the expression on her face was one of puzzlement.

"Then Smythe wasn't perfect."

"No." Her skin started turning deep red at her thoughts. And then, abruptly, she fell back against the dirt, her body trembling. She looked more vulnerable than before as she clasped her hands together and held them out before her. "Oh, Almighty God, give me a portion of the faith You bestowed upon Your prophet, J'Sopah Smythe. I will work so much harder to be worthy of Thee, to do whatever acts You would have me commit in Your Holy Name. If I have offended Thee in any way, please rebuke and cleanse me. I want to be worthy of Thy blessings."

Finally she was through, and stood.

"It is not your very large and strong body that could ever keep us apart, dear Neshi. I crave the pleasures we could share together. Neshi, it is your mind, your soul, the residue of your past that forms the only real barrier between us."

Tuati walked back to the village, leaving him there by the pure azure water.

He sat, looking around, seeing the clear sky, smelling the air laced with a hundred scents.

J'Sopah Smythe—he had been hearing a great deal about this individual. Everyone on Nede seemed to have his name on their lips throughout each day.

They spoke as much about him as they did about this so-called God they were supposed to be worshiping—often more. They had Smythe's rules and regulations, trusting him to have presented these to all of them exactly as they had been given to him by God.

Logic suggested that he could have mistranslated one rule, a dozen, a hundred.

Or maybe this was his way of controlling an entire race long after his death, *and any supposed contact with God was only a game, a game that might have been played by the Natasians!*

The similarity struck him almost physically. He recalled how, on his world, a shadow government had passed through flesh-and-blood puppets a whole library of guidelines for daily living, laws by which generations had been governed. That was, in fact, the nature of his work as a Tech Detective, to enforce the many laws and arrest those in violation.

Here, on Nede, J'Sopah Smythe was long gone, but his legacy remained well entrenched. Neshi shivered suddenly, though the afternoon temperature was quite moderate. He looked again at what Tuati had written in the dirt: *Satan.*

On Neshi's world and on others he had visited, there was always the same spirit of darkness, the same manifestations of despair. Yet here on Nede, there seemed only health, happiness, vibrancy.

Had the other societies started out akin to the way this one was functioning?

What had gone wrong? What had taken away their abundance and joy?

29

Dwaun showed him the settlement's library. "Many of the volumes have turned to dust over the years, unfortunately," he said with great sorrow. "But virtually all of their contents have been transcribed to newer ones. Still, it's a pity."

"The books of J'Sopah Smythe," Neshi said. "May I see them?"

"Oh, yes!" Dwaun replied excitedly. "Are you interested in becoming one of us?"

"We shall see."

The library was two stories high, as primitive in construction as the rest of the buildings. The books were arranged on wooden shelves, categorized systematically. One whole section was devoted to the writings of J'Sopah Smythe.

"I'll leave you alone," Dwaun said in a kindly tone. "Take as long as you like."

Neshi sat on the floor. The wicker chairs in the library had been made for the much lighter Nedians; his girth and weight would collapse any of them in an instant.

Neshi read through book after book.

There was much that was beautiful in the writings Smythe had left behind, much indeed.

"I saw His shining angel stand in front of me and a smile cross that wondrous face. The sounds of trumpets filled the air, the scent of jasmine touched my nostrils."

Neshi was beguiled by the mental image that had formed.

"I felt the joy of being so near to one of His beautiful winged creations, unspoiled by the ravages of sin."

But there were others that Neshi didn't react to in the same way, a far more negative impression arising.

"I stood with Almighty God on the pinnacle of a mountain. I looked over all of creation. I saw His handiwork throughout the heavens. And I knew He had chosen me as a vessel, a vessel of redemption."

The arrogance in that statement wasn't lost on Neshi.

"Almighty God has given us a Book of Laws by which my kind shall be guided. It is to be His Plan for every aspect of their lives. By listening to Him through me, they will be able to earn the salvation that only He can provide. Without obedience, they are doomed. They will go on not to an eternal life of majesty but one of unending torment. They must listen to me. Almighty God has proclaimed this. They must accept every syllable."

Neshi nearly skipped the rest of that particular passage, thinking how absurd such a vision was, how self-deluding. And to realize that it had been foisted upon an entire race!

But there was more: "I am to become His sole representative on this planet. I am to rule, as though I were Almighty God Himself, and they are to come to me in worship and obedience. Before my Book of Laws, there is to be no other."

He was becoming disgusted. How could the Nedians be so blind, so foolish, so unquestioning?

Neshi spent the remainder of the afternoon in the library, reading book after book. When he had finished, he leaned back against the wall and considered what he had read.

It was empty, glittering on the surface, full of hope and faith, but inside, deep in the core, everything was dependent upon a flesh-and-blood member of a mortal race and his alleged revelations from a divine source.

Oblivious to this, Dwaun and Graita and Tuati and the others had accepted J'Sopah Smythe as their prophet. In their eyes he was holy and divine, having passed from the physical and corruptible into the spiritual and the immortal.

Into the spiritual and the immortal, like the Currents of the Cosmos, but with the full retention of personality and total awareness.

"I am dying, I know. As my eyes close and I feel mortality seeping from me like wine from a leaking cask, I am entering what I have prophesied for so long. I am entering the next life, I am joining—the darkness! The flames! I am—"

There had been scribes sitting at Smythe's deathbed. They took down every word, preserved every syllable for the perpetual use of his followers.

" . . . the darkness . . . the flames."

The Nedians explained those harsh words as Smythe's way of saying that the precepts he had taught, the ones that had been given him in an endless series of visions over the years, had been true and had enabled him to avoid the punishment reserved for Satan, which was eternal fire and torment.

Neshi wasn't so sure. He didn't know what else they could signify but something inside him, some knot of disbelief, made him look at those last words of a dying Nedian in a different light, and it filled him with the same sort of chill he had felt after sending Ferene's body out into utter nothingness.

30

Tuati invited Neshi to a ceremony. "You are consumed with doubt," she said. "You must see what gives us such faith."

The ceremony was to take place that evening in the community's circular hub. Everyone would be taking part.

Neshi decided to spend the time until then in the library or off by himself, thinking. He read more books, more facts about the existence of that world and the society that had formed on it.

So similar even amidst the differences. That thought struck him again and again, but never more forcefully than when he read one particular passage: "The original settlers came here from elsewhere."

He repeated the words out loud: "The original settlers came here from elsewhere!" That was how it all had commenced on his home world.

"They fought against the most awful conditions and carved out a life for themselves that was tolerable. Eventually the weather changed. The monstrous creatures afflicting them died off. They were able to build a society based upon life given from the soil."

That was the difference. Neshi's race went industrial, while Tuati's traveled an agricultural route.

For those who are farmers, it is only logical to look to some Being in the sky, born of their own flesh-and-blood needs, Neshi reasoned. *But my kind made our own machines, our own laws. We took control and did not need—*

He stopped himself. *We took control.*

He shook his head a couple of times, as if by that action he could get his thoughts more sharply in focus.

Did we? he asked himself. *How much in control were we?*

The Natasians weren't some nebulous spirit in the sky, but they were not of flesh and bone and blood, either.

He sighed wearily as he tried to piece together the connection, if there was one. Or could it be that the circumstances on each world were totally separate tableaus, with no unifying thread whatever?

Yet there was unification of a sort—the universal destruction he found everywhere, with only this present world, this planet called Nede, having escaped thus far. Galaxy after galaxy of nothing but the shells of former civilizations now dust.

He shivered deeply. It was just what he had been taught since shortly after birth: life was all there was, and the Currents of the Cosmos, as vague as that had been, as impersonal and uncomforting, was nothing but a pitiable attempt to—

A burst of insight hit him.

Yes!

The Nedian approach was the next step!

He stood suddenly and started pacing, not aware that others were looking at him curiously. They had simply gone beyond formless nothingness to a view that promised another *life!*

His shoulders sank. *An evolution toward truth, or yet another delusion imposed by fear of dying?*

He left the library quickly and walked outside, down one of the dusty streets to the outskirts. Stretching out before him was a forest that began at the northern edge of the village. To the west was farmland; to the east, the azure lake.

The Nedians weren't vegetarians; they caught fish in the lake and hunted game in the forest. Together with the crops they raised, they had no worries about feeding themselves.

He looked up at the sky. "I'm supposed to meet You tonight," he said. "The trouble is that I cannot accept You as real. If You *are* real, then why did you allow the Natasians such control? Why didn't You step in before it was too late?"

His only answer was the howling of some creature in the forest directly ahead.

The Nedian night came from the east to the west, like a blanket pulled over the planet. Earlier that evening, Neshi had stood in the middle of one of the wider streets and had the unique experience of seeing one side in darkness and the other still lit by the fleeting rays of Nede's sun. This effect lasted mere seconds, and then nighttime started to cover everything.

He had been in the hut assigned to him only a short

while when he heard Tuati approach the hut and gently rap on the door.

"Come in," Neshi said.

She entered and smiled as she saw him staring at her. "You act as though this is the first time you've seen me," she said.

"It might as well be," he told her.

She was dressed in a multicolored garment made entirely out of flowers, a dozen or more hues woven together. On the top of her head was a crown of the blossoms.

Neshi reached out a hand toward her, touching her cheek with infinite tenderness. "So beautiful," he remarked. "So much like—"

"Etarina?"

"Yes! How did you know?"

"When you first came here, you kept saying her name over and over. And another."

"Yes," he said, blushing a bit with embarrassment.

"Baba. Baba."

"Her nickname for me."

"Nickname?"

"A cute little personal name, known only to us. Very, very special."

Tuati smiled again. "Do you want a nickname from me?" she asked.

"I would be delighted."

"Ma'Tu."

"Ma'Tu. Ma'Tu." He repeated it, enjoying the sound.

"It means gift of God," Tuati remarked.

"Gift of God?"

"Yes. You may not believe in Him, but not believing in

the sun or the moon does nothing to remove them from their orbits."

"I would like to, Tuati. I would like to believe everything you do. But I've seen too much that disputes His existence. I cannot toss all that away or be expected to ignore it from now on." He tapped his temple. "It's up here. It's in my mind. My brain has recorded every detail, Tuati. And what I have seen out there," he waved his hand toward the sky, "proves that only mindless chance exists. Any good, any happiness, any nobility is isolated, Tuati. Isolated and rare. Where it exists somehow, it dies out eventually, its ashes mocking any who later walk through them."

"And *we* are doomed, Neshi? Are you saying that?"

"Please," he said. "I know this is a special night. I am looking forward to sharing it with you."

A single tear trickled down her nearly transparent cheek like a drop of rain on a windowpane.

"Say good-bye to me, Neshi," she said.

"You must leave now?"

She nodded, a strange expression on her face. "I have to go and prepare. The ceremony begins in a very short while. Please, Neshi, say good-bye."

He reached out, and they tenderly embraced.

"You're trembling," he said. "Why are you trembling?"

There was more than one tear now; there were many tears.

"You don't have to water these flowers," he joked. "They seem healthy enough."

"Healthy now, yes, but then they wither and die, and the wind carries each petal away."

She turned to leave. "Ma'Tu," she said, savoring the name. "Yes, that is exactly right."

She whispered something as she shut the door behind her. He almost missed the words, they were spoken so softly. "Ma'Tu. Gift of God. If only you believed in Him."

He could have been irritated, could have felt more than a little offended that she would continue to throw an idiotic belief system at him.

He wasn't.

She had seemed so fragile then, her tone pleading, that he felt ashamed at his reluctance.

31

Each Nedian held a candle. Every avenue leading into the central hub was jammed with them, creating a symphony of light.

The effect at dusk was breathtaking.

"Quite beautiful, isn't it?" Dwaun remarked.

"Yes." Neshi answered him softly, the images filling him with an almost worshipful feeling.

They were standing just inside the hub and could see 360 degrees.

"Occasionally, when Etarina and I would stand outside, looking up at the sky, we would talk about the vastness. I have now traveled through a portion of that sea of space, as one of our philosophers called it, and have seen nothing but misery."

"Misery because God wasn't at the center," Dwaun replied. "But He's never very far away, waiting."

"But if God were out there at all, He must have been hiding. I didn't see Him."

"Do you see the oxygen we breathe?"

"No, of course not."

"But you believe in it, don't you?"

"Yes, but—"

"If suddenly you were gasping for air, what would you say?"

"That something had happened to the supply of oxygen."

Dwaun smiled, pleased with himself. "So it is only when you *experience* the oxygen that you believe it is there. Is that right?"

"Dwaun, I don't see—" Neshi started to say, but then Dwaun's point became clear.

A recollection from his home world rose to the surface of his mind.

The male had been a smoker virtually all of his adult life. He was now gasping for air. Etarina and Neshi had been out walking that evening. The male approached them, his face contorted with pain.

He fell inches away from them. Inside of a minute or two, he had experienced a massive heart attack and died.

Later they found that the smoking had so damaged his lungs and strained his heart that he was literally suffocating. The oxygen was all around him, but the choice to smoke had caused blockage.

Neshi told Dwaun what he had remembered.

"That is exactly what I've been trying to say," Dwaun replied. "God is *here*, Neshi. He really is. But we make a decision to receive Him or we go on living in a way that blocks His entry into our very beings."

Neshi shook himself. "Still nonsense," he said without convincing either Dwaun or himself.

"It's time," the other said.

"How can you tell?"

"Look."

Neshi saw a strangely familiar sight: shapes, very faint at first, like fireflies over the moors at night.

A chill gripped him, a feeling of repetition, like reliving a once-played but forgotten scene.

"They are the angels of Almighty God," Dwaun whispered.

"What are they waiting for?" Neshi asked.

He saw the answer a millisecond later.

Tuati emerged into the hub. She walked directly to the center. Her head turned slightly toward him. He saw her lips move, and then she lifted her hands, palms upward, toward the hovering shapes.

A second passed, then another. It seemed everything had been suspended, frozen in time.

Then the Almighty God of the Nedians appeared, and Neshi recognized him in an instant.

He had come from the opposite end of the room, lumbering toward him, a creature three times his height. Its feet were cloven hooves, its hands like talons, its face lined with boils, the flesh green and yellow.

"Isn't He glorious?" Dwaun commented in awe, an oddly hollow sound to his voice, as though he was talking by rote.

"Glorious?" Neshi said with utter astonishment. "That monster?"

Dwaun turned sharply and glowered at Neshi. "How can you say that about our Almighty God? How dare you speak such blasphemy?" Dwaun returned to the sight confronting them, doing so in a manner that was a clear rejection of Neshi's existence at that moment.

Neshi looked at the faces of the other Nedians within sight.

So happy, he thought. *So unaware! Especially Tuati.*

She stood before the figure hovering above her, then that figure began descending toward her.

As Neshi started to run ahead to stop her, Dwaun grabbed hold of him. "No!" he yelled. "You mustn't!"

"That thing is going to kill her!"

"That is what she *wants*," Dwaun screamed. "That is how much she loves you."

"Are you saying that the only time your Almighty God appears is when He can take a sacrifice?"

"It is more than that," Dwaun said desperately. "It is not death. It is new life—in *Him!*"

Tuati turned and looked toward him a final time. "Neshi, she wanted you to see the reality of our Almighty God," Dwaun said, sobbing. "If it took her life to accomplish this, that was the price she was willing to pay!"

Neshi stood, transfixed, as the creature worked its way with that pale, fragile body, her screams of pain quickly dying, until nothing remained.

Finally the creature faced Neshi, an apparent look of disdain on that awful face, followed by another expression, one that smacked of fear. And then it was gone.

32

Neshi lay in his hut, shivering, images of that awful creature pummeling his mind.

Tuati had been absorbed molecule by molecule, just as his soldiers had been at Asframore. Her head was the last part of her body to go, her lips stretched wide in a cry of torment.

She died for me, he told himself. *She sacrificed her life that I might believe.*

He shivered more severely then.

She never knew that I had met this so-called Almighty God before.

He jumped to his feet.

"I want to meet you again!" he screamed. "I want to face you. I want to destroy you."

And yet he realized that nothing he could do would

ever doom such an elusive enemy, a thing of mind and spirit, not flesh and blood.

He dropped, sobbing, back to the ground.

Dwaun came to his hut in the morning.

"I know what a shock it must have been."

His tone was sincere, the words spoken earnestly, but Neshi noticed something else—a measure of impatience.

Dwaun sat down beside him.

"Tuati loved you," he said. "I have never seen such a love before."

"I have known it once before now," Neshi told him.

"Yes. Etarina."

"They were very similar. Neither knew what it was like not to be devoted."

"And both were taken from you."

Neshi's eyes peered into Dwaun's own. "Etarina was taken from me. Tuati was *thrown away*."

"How can you still say that?"

"I can still say it because it is a fact."

"Always the rationalist!"

"Always one who values truth."

"You *saw* truth out there a few hours ago. How more starkly could truth be presented to you, Neshi?"

Something about Dwaun seemed vaguely artificial.

"That was delusion, Dwaun. That was the delusion of a race held captive by a monstrous creature whose very nature is evil and who has somehow tricked you into thinking it is the essence of all that is good and wonderful."

Both got to their feet.

"*You* are the one under delusion," Dwaun said, practically spitting the words at him. "You take that which is

224

holy and wonderful and treat it as though it is dung into which you have accidentally stepped."

Neshi's tone changed, his eyes welling up with moisture. "Is it holy, Dwaun? Is it wonderful when a sweet and innocent being like Tuati can be peeled away, inch by inch, layer by layer, until not even her molecules are left, sucked into the maw of a—"

"*No!*" Dwaun screamed. "You are a devil! You see in the Almighty that which you yourself have become." He walked quickly to the doorway and stood there, his back to Neshi, his body shuddering with the effort he had to exert to bring himself under control. Without turning, he said, "You are to leave us, Neshi. You are to go elsewhere, spreading your poison there but leaving us alone! I only hope—"

He cut himself off and started to walk down the street.

Neshi ran after him. "What good would that do, Dwaun? Everywhere on this planet it is the same. The ideas of J'Sopah Smythe permeate this society at every level. I could go to another village, but it would be the same. Others like Tuati sacrificing themselves for no reason. Your Almighty God is *never* going to be satisfied. All of you could throw yourselves at him, and still that would not be enough. That foul creature would go to another planet and then another. I *know!* I have *seen* the husks of once-vibrant worlds left in its wake."

Dwaun swung at him, connecting with his jaw, but the blow was like a feather, hardly felt. Dwaun swung again and again, until his knuckles were bloody. The final time, Neshi reached out and grabbed him by the wrists.

"You are so helpless here in so many ways, Dwaun," he said, not unkindly. "You have only to wait your turn at

some ghastly feast, beings herded together for the plea-
sure of a creature who wants only to consume you, to suck
in every cell of your body."

Dwaun pulled away. "Even if what you say is true, then
how many in this universe or any of the other universes
out there—"

He swung one hand painfully toward the sky.

"—ever manage to escape the destiny that has been
theirs from the beginning?"

"It is your destiny only to die, Dwaun. It is *not* your
destiny to squander life in some kind of perverted worship
ceremony."

"May Almighty God forgive you for that."

"May I one day stand again before this creature and
plunge a dagger into whatever he or it has that passes for
a heart!"

Dwaun backed away, though not in fear. Disgust was
on his face, and a trace of pity. "You are to leave by midday tomorrow," he said solemnly.

"But where will I go?" Neshi asked, a note of despera-
tion in his voice.

"Where you came from!" Dwaun pointed toward the sky.

Later that day, Graita found Neshi sitting by the azure
lake.

"Dwaun is sorry he spoke so strongly," she said.

"Dwaun is not here to tell me himself," Neshi observed.

"He is proud. It is difficult for him." She was sitting
beside him, looking so much like Tuati.

He bowed his head, trying to fight back some very
strong emotions.

Graita reached out and touched his shoulder as she
spoke. "She wanted so much for you to believe."

226

He looked up. "But I saw what this Almighty God of yours looked like. I have seen him before, Graita, as he really is."

"Yes, I know."

"But you continue to hang onto—"

"Not any longer, Neshi," she interrupted.

He could scarcely believe what she had just said. He was about to ask her what had happened when she reached out and touched his lips with the fingers of her left hand.

"Later, my friend."

"Later? What is going on, Graita?"

"Dwaun is packing some things."

"What do you mean?"

She smiled again. "My beloved will explain."

"We had such harsh words between us."

"He reacted as a follower of J'Sopah Smythe."

"And now?"

"As your friend."

Impulsively he reached out and hugged her. She blushed in a pink wave from head to foot.

33

Neshi, Graita, and Dwaun had walked some distance from the village, at first without talking, wounded emotions still present. Ahead was the western tip of a mountain range that went on for hundreds of miles.

"Just beyond," Dwaun said succinctly, a large leather sack swung over his shoulder.

Neshi nodded.

It wasn't much of a climb. They reached a small plateau just below the top before Neshi turned and confronted Dwaun.

"I do not have to leave," he remarked.

Dwaun looked at him intently. "Neshi, you said that without thinking."

"No."

"You *did* say it without thinking. You cannot stay here. How could you, after seeing what you did?"

Neshi hesitated. What Dwaun had just spoken was true, yet he found the reality of it maddening.

"But how can I go?" he asked. "How can I leave to go again out there?" He looked up at the clear afternoon sky, his body trembling. "I have seen worlds become tombs. I have—"

His voice broke.

Graita reached out and put her arm around him. "In time it will be no different here," she said softly. "We have seen the Almighty, the truth of what he is. We believe that Nede will eventually be like all the others."

"I don't want to hear," Neshi replied. "I can no longer face the emptiness."

Dwaun stood in front of Neshi.

"Listen!" he pleaded.

"Your Almighty God is a monster!" Neshi blurted. "Your Almighty God—"

"We *know!* We saw him as he really is last night. Listen to what I'm saying, Neshi!"

Neshi looked up, the words finally penetrating the mental haze into which he had slipped.

"Its feet were cloven hooves," Dwaun continued, "its hands like talons, its face lined with boils, the flesh green and yellow."

Neshi's eyes widened in astonishment.

"You saw that I was telling the truth!" he said.

Both Graita and Dwaun nodded.

"But you seemed so certain that I was deceiving myself," Neshi reminded them both. "Why didn't you tell me everything?"

Dwaun looked helpless, throwing his hands out in confusion. "It was only a glimpse, Neshi. Not from the beginning, as with you. Before that, Tuati spoke, her words cutting into my brain."

"You *heard* her?"

"Yes. We all are closely attuned."

"Remember when you thought I had read your mind earlier?" Graita spoke up.

He did.

"It is like that, a special sensitivity toward one another," she added.

"What did Tuati say?" Neshi asked.

"*Satan.* Just that one name, that one awful name."

Dwaun stopped for a few minutes, then continued. "It was then that I saw what you did, a truth shared with us by Tuati, who had broken through the facade erected in our minds over the years."

"And me, too," Graita said. "We knew, then, that we had been worshiping Satan from the beginning."

"But you've not told me why you lied," Neshi reminded them.

"I couldn't admit it to myself at first," Dwaun replied. "I thought I had had some kind of delusion."

"Caused by Satan," Graita added.

"Yes, caused by Satan," Dwaun agreed. "But then Graita saw what I did. And you."

Dwaun was like a child then, ashamed but also deeply fearful. "Years of faith, of hope. Years of everything upon which my kind have built our society, ripped away before our eyes." He motioned for Graita to continue.

"Dwaun came to me only minutes after the ceremony had ended and everyone else had returned to their homes," Graita went on. "I thought he was dying of some spasm. We both shared the same torment."

"But why last night?" Neshi puzzled. "Why not a year ago? A decade ago! Why now?"

"There was only one element different last night," Graita said. She smiled as she looked directly at him. "You, Neshi. You were there. Not a year ago, not ten years ago, but last night you were. It's something to do with you."

That revelation swept the breath from him, and he had to sit down on the bare rock plateau, his mind whirling with confusion.

Long ago he had been called to command a rebel army, proclaimed the messiah who was destined to lead them to victory. Again, his very existence had been elevated to some kind of pedestal!

"And that is why you carry that sack, with things for my journey?" he asked moments later.

Graita and Dwaun stood before him, looking expectantly at him. "Things for *our* journey, Neshi," they said in unison.

He jumped to his feet. "You two are coming with me?"

"Yes!" Graita said triumphantly.

"We want to go wherever your own destiny leads," Dwaun added. "We will live or die by your side."

Countless questions begged to be asked and answered. What about their fellow Nedians? Why were Graita and Dwaun leaving without apparent compunction? It was a moment so charged with emotion that rational, objective, incisive Neshi threw a lifetime of upbringing and training aside, and they hugged for the joy of it.

After a few minutes, they climbed to the top and Neshi looked out over a plain in the middle of which rested the vessel that had taken him across the reaches of more than one unknown galaxy.

34

Storyteller paused and recognized someone who had raised a hand. "Yes," he said. "You have a question?"

The other replied, "It makes little sense, Storyteller. Graita and Dwaun have decided to throw away everything and go with Neshi. Is it logical that they would do so?"

"Is reality always logical, my friend? Are flesh-and-blood creations so predictable that they might as well be robots, which act only on the basis of carefully programmed logic?"

"But what caused them to suddenly leave?"

"Graita and Dwaun saw a change in those around them, an unfriendliness replacing their earlier sense of hospitality, of simple courtesy, and such, this taking place after Tuati's sacrifice."

"What was the rest? That in itself isn't sufficient."

"That is what Dwaun will reveal to Neshi a short while after they have taken off from the planet."

"I am eager to hear, Storyteller. We all are."

"And I am eager to tell it."

The questioner sat down and listened as intently as those around him.

35

"We could sense something being altered within our fellow Nedians," Dwaun was saying as Graita and he regained control of their emotions after experiencing takeoff and their first thrust into space. "This was quickly reflected in their physical appearance."

"It was changing?" Neshi asked.

"Dramatically!"

"In so short a time?"

"That is correct."

Neshi and Dwaun were sitting on the floor of the cramped control quarters.

"Neshi, their attitudes, their behavior, even the pigmentation of their skin was being rapidly altered," Dwaun continued. "Several told Graita and me of intense pain in their bodies, in the area of their hearts and their stomachs, as though someone had grabbed hold of those organs and was squeezing them unmercifully."

"Dying?"

"Perhaps, Neshi, perhaps. Or experiencing some new and terrible sickness. Whatever the case, there would seem to be two possible causes." He paused briefly, turning his head toward the ceiling of the compartment. "Both are connected with you."

"Me? I don't understand."

"The first is the possibility that you brought in some disease from your wanderings, and that Graita and I will eventually fall prey to the same organisms."

"What about the other?"

"That you planted the seed of doubt. You started the corrosion of their faith."

"But it was faith in evil, faith in Satan."

"Oh, yes, Graita and I realize that now. But Neshi, they have nothing with which to replace it. They have no foundation for their lives."

"But you two are here. You didn't succumb."

"You are speaking the truth."

"Why didn't you become part of what was happening to them? What was different about the two of you?"

"We saw something else that night, in addition to what you saw," Graita said.

"What was it?"

"Beautiful luminescent creatures. They were hovering near—" She was overcome with emotion, burying her head in her hands.

Dwaun stood and put his arms around her. "They were so fine, Neshi. They had such peace on their faces— sublime peace. They looked at us with such undeserved love. They seemed to be reaching out toward us."

"But Satan did not react. It was as though they weren't there at all," Neshi replied.

Graita looked up. "You are very wrong," she said. "You are very wrong, Neshi. He disappeared seconds later *because of them!*"

"Yes, I saw that," Neshi interrupted, a bit impatiently. "He disappeared right after he had taken Tuati."

"No, dear friend! After *they* had taken her!"

Neshi leaned back against the metallic wall of the compartment. "I saw Tuati eaten alive by that monster. How can you say that?"

"Her body," Dwaun spoke up. "Her body was eaten, but not the eternal part of her."

An invisible stream somewhere beyond time and space, millions of formless consciousnesses adrift in it, countless more being ingested with each passing day.

"I know! I know!" Neshi said, his voice getting louder and louder. "The Currents of the Cosmos. Etarina's supposed to be part of it. I know all about it!"

"You do not," Graita said finally, wiping her eyes, her voice quiet but commanding. She sat down in front of Neshi, taking his hands into her own. "All of us know just a piece of the truth. What I saw on Tuati's face told me in that moment that she knew at least some of the rest. The abyss that extends beyond this life, Neshi, was no longer there for Tuati. She had had a veil pulled from her vision. She saw no darkness, Neshi, but blazing, wonderful light. It shone on her face as the winged creatures took her away from Satan's grasp."

"If the winged ones hadn't appeared, what would Satan have done?"

"Taken his next sacrifices," Dwaun replied.

"What would have satisfied Satan until the next time? Where was it to have ended?"

Dwaun had come to Graita's side again. They were holding hands. "With us, dear friend," he said. "With us."

Neshi could not speak.

"We promised Tuati that if it took more than her death, we were willing."

"We were ready," Graita added. "We wouldn't have hesitated. That was why Dwaun acted so strongly."

Dwaun leaned forward, taking Neshi's head in his hands and looking directly into his eyes. "She said something else," Dwaun added. "Just a name. It was like no other in memory."

"Both of you heard this?" Neshi asked haltingly.

"Yes, we did," he heard Graita say.

"What was that name?"

Dwaun smiled. "*Jesus*," he said. "She was saying hello to someone named Jesus."

36

They spent much of the journey in hibernation. The food they brought with them would last only a short while. Hibernation had been, for Neshi, a taste of what he thought death was going to be like, a kind of pseudo-oblivion, devoid of the normal senses, and with devastating near totality, yet with a vague and contradictory awareness of existence. They would climb into their tubular containers, close the lids, and be enveloped by a special gas that would suspend them between full, functioning life and total, irreversible death.

That first time, so long ago, as science was doing its work on him, he recalled realizing how strange it was that there were three hibernation containers, not two or four, but three. When that fact hit him originally, he had just sent Ferene's body out into space, turned from the portal, and looked at the two containers next to the one he would use.

Three was exactly the number needed, as it had turned out.

How could the Natasians have known? They might be evil incarnate, but surely they were not omniscient. The thought of that potentiality filled him with a dread that was stark and awful.

For a moment, as unconsciousness spread over him—not unpleasantly, not even abruptly, more a gradual surrendering to the darkness, like reentering his mother's womb—he wondered if the Natasians in fact had *anything* to do with what was happening now. Suddenly, just before the nothingness came, he heard a sound, the sound of someone humming a strange, lilting melody, so sweet, so beautiful that it carried him into the abyss with an unaccustomed peace.

Even with hibernation, they were growing increasingly weak, because they had programmed their containers to release them periodically. Otherwise they might end up in a ship so damaged by galactic debris that its systems might fail and they might die.

And so their biosystems normalized, which meant they experienced the customary requirements for food and liquids, and their supplies, even with the replenishment brought from Nede, dwindled to a point where they had only a few portions left.

Ahead. . . .

Directly ahead of them: a planet.

There had been other planets since they left Nede, always pale and dreary orbs with dry, dead surfaces that gave no hint of any of the elements necessary to support life—one global coffin after another, driving home the truths Neshi had been trying to tell them all along.

"Nothing!" Dwaun had exclaimed. "Is it God's idea of creation to make only empty husks?"

"Not quite," Neshi had said, surprised that he had slipped into the position of being God's defense counsel. "We see only what they have become. A thousand, a million, a hundred million years before our journey past them, they may have been quite different, perhaps pure and thriving with life."

"Like Nede," Dwaun said.

"Yes, I imagine so."

"What happened, do you think?"

"The races living on them became corrupt."

"Through Satan? As we suspect is now the case with Nede?"

"Yes, possibly through what you call Satan."

"And God rained judgment on them."

"That is one way of looking at it."

Graita spoke, minutes after they were confronted by a totally different image beyond the ship. "Then how do we explain that?" she asked, pointing at what they saw through the window in the control cabin.

How indeed? Here was a world with a surface of stretches of green, suggesting possibly fertile land, and other patches that hinted at vast expanses of water.

"It's the only world we've seen with such textures of color," Graita added. "The only world thus far where we have any hope of—"

The ship lurched as it entered the planet's gravitational field.

"Won't you pray, Neshi?" she asked. "Won't you please pray?"

"How can I engage in a privilege I have done nothing to earn?" he asked pointedly.

"You can simply—" she started to say, then stopped herself, realizing that everything she had been taught from childhood supported Neshi's question but not her aborted answer. For the moment, she could not cope with that puzzling abstract in the very eminent reality of a landing that would either spare them for a new chapter in their odyssey or splatter them on the surface of an unknown and puzzling anachronism—a planet apparently alive, the only one apart from Nede in the vastness of space, with little hope of it ever, ever being different, little hope of anything but the bones of countless civilizations awaiting their hapless passage.

Part Four

Death be not proud, though some have called thee
Mighty and dreadful, for thou art not so,
For those whom thou think'st thou dost overthrow,
Die not, poor death, not yet canst thou kill me.

JOHN DONNE

37

The landing was far worse than Neshi's had proved to be on Nede.

Graita died.

38

Dwaun and Neshi looked at their surroundings.

They were in a valley. Tall mountain peaks rose north and west. Everywhere they turned, they could see trees, bushes, lush growth, seemingly without end.

"Listen!" Neshi said.

The musical sound of birds.

Dwaun sank to his knees. They had just buried his beloved, bowing their heads and whispering good-bye to her.

"She was so kind, so sweet," Dwaun sobbed. "And now—"

Neshi joined him. "I do understand, my good friend."

Dwaun looked at him. "Etarina?"

"Yes," Neshi said slowly. "Yes, Etarina."

Dwaun had never been told the full story, so Neshi decided to let him know everything.

"They did that to her?" Dwaun said, astonished.

"Oh, they did. They switched her brain back and forth. They kept her consciousness alive for a very long time."

Tears were pouring down her cheeks.

He wiped them away with a paper tissue from a pocket in his uniform, but they kept coming.

She couldn't speak anymore, that one precious word having taken all her strength. Abruptly she started coughing, a racking cough that was tearing her up inside. Several of the wires attached to her body were ripped out, and blood began to color the white sheet.

"She wanted me to kill her, to end her misery, to break the awful chain of bodies," Neshi sobbed.

"What happened?"

He saw in her eyes a pleading that he could not ignore, could not resist. As he stood back, took the pistol, and aimed it at her, for a fleeting instant there was something else in her eyes, a fading reminder of the love they once—

He never got the chance.

His beloved smiled so very briefly, then her head turned slightly to one side and her eyes closed.

"She smiled, Dwaun! She smiled amidst all that pain!"

"Just like Graita!"

How true that was. They had pulled Graita from the wreckage, her pale body smeared with blood, so many bones broken that she seemed like a very limp doll. But she was not quite dead. They had made her as comfortable as possible, putting some soft moss under her head, Dwaun holding one hand, Neshi the other.

She had only a few minutes left.

"I have no fear," she had whispered. "I have no fear, my beloved mate, my beloved friend."

She smiled.

"Isn't that wonderful?" she said joyously. "Satan is vanquished. He really is!"

She closed her eyes momentarily and they thought she was gone, but those pale lids with long black lashes opened one more time.

"Something else," she said.

Amazingly she was able to pull gently away from both of them and sit up. She stretched out her hands, palms upward.

"There's a last chance," she said. "There's a last chance for everyone. Reject it, and there are only flames forever."

As she started to fall backward, they supported her with their hands, and she rested again on the moss.

"Listen," she said, her voice nearly gone. "Listen within you while there is time. He comes to you with love, and then His angels lift you up, up, up. It's so beautiful, it—"

Her eyes closed. Her breathing stopped.

"*Graita!*" Dwaun's cry had torn through the valley and echoed off the mountains.

39

They stayed in that valley for days, eating wild fruit, trapping animals and roasting them over fires.

"I did this more than once on my world," Neshi recalled. "I would go out into the moors for days at a time, chasing lawbreakers. My food would run out, forcing me to eat whatever was available."

"And what was that?" Dwaun asked.

Neshi started to describe some of the creatures.

"Enough!" Dwaun exclaimed. "It sounds worse than on Nede."

Each day, Dwaun would go to where Graita was buried and just stand there, his head bowed, sometimes weeping, sometimes with little emotion at all.

"She said He comes to us with love. That seems a contradiction," Neshi observed one day.

"To what?"

"To what she also said—that if we reject Him, there are only flames forever. How can God love on the one hand and torment with eternal flames on the other?" Neshi asked. "I was taught that we all went into the same universal melting pot, without some kind of eternal vengeance."

Dwaun raised his head and looked at his friend. "But is that fair?" he inquired.

"How do you mean that?"

"Is it fair that Graita and Tuati and Etarina should end up in the same melting pot as those who served the Natasians so well, as those who were in such close allegiance with Satan?"

"But we have no control over that."

"You're wrong, Neshi. To a very real extent we *do* determine what happens."

Neshi was sensitive to the tragedy Dwaun had faced, so his normal penchant for debate and rebuttal were restrained.

"Let's talk later," he said.

Dwaun nodded, surrendering to his grief again.

Neshi went off by himself to explore the territory, leaving Dwaun behind.

"I just want to stay here, near her," the other said, then quickly added, "I know she isn't here, but her flesh is all that I knew, all that I could touch and hold, and it's so hard, Neshi, so hard for me to let go of her completely. I'm not ready for that, my friend."

Neshi found the cabin after about an hour's walk.

It was empty, seemingly abandoned, the front door slightly ajar. He walked inside. Some food remained in a plate on top of a table that appeared to have been handmade.

There were books on a shelf. He read the titles. "How could that be?" he asked out loud. This was an alien world, a different culture. But then so had been all the others, including Nede—and he had understood the language in each case, whether in decaying libraries or in the tongue spoken by the Nedians.

He picked out one of the books and started to leaf through it.

Noise outside.

He ran to the door, dropping the book on the floor. A figure was stumbling along the dirt path leading to the cabin. A male!

He fell at Neshi's feet. "Please help me," he said. "I know you're there."

His head turned upward. The eyes had been seared with flame, burned sightless!

Neshi took the male in his arms and pulled him into the cabin.

"They wanted to make sure I couldn't identify them," the man said. "They took everything from me. All my money! I was going to put it away in the bank. I was—"

He was on the verge of passing out.

Neshi put him gently on what must have been a bed, then found a cloth and dampened it with cold water from a faucet in the kitchen.

Rubbing the cloth across the male's forehead seemed to relieve him a bit.

"They took my sight!" he exclaimed. "They used a cigarette lighter and—and took my sight."

"Where can I get help?" Neshi asked.

"Your voice! So deep. That accent!"

"Please tell me, where can I go?"

"Nowhere. We have nowhere to turn."

"But that cannot be!"

"There is a village just south of here." The male coughed with pain. "But it will do no good," he said. "They are hateful."

Neshi started to pull away from him.

"Get my Bible," the male said. "I want at least to hold it."

"Your Bible?"

"Yes, it's got a black leather cover. On the shelf over there."

Neshi looked on the shelf, then glanced down at the volume he'd dropped minutes before: *Holy Bible.*

"Why is it called *Holy*?" he asked.

"Because it is from God," the male replied. "Please, hand it to me."

Neshi picked it up and took it over to the male.

"God'll be with me while you're gone, my friend. Please be very careful. You are in a dangerous place."

"Where was your God when you were attacked?"

"Getting ready to welcome me into His Kingdom."

Neshi shrugged his shoulders and left. In an hour or so, he had found his way to the outskirts of the village, a primitive, isolated place of simple wood buildings.

No one walked the streets. Music was coming from a building with a steeple on the top.

Neshi approached it. Peering through one of the side windows, he saw that there were males and females inside, with pale skin like the one in the cabin, the males with bare heads shaven of hair.

They were dressed quite neatly, though plainly, and they seemed well-scrubbed.

He looked at his hands—dirty—felt his face—a beard. He sniffed the air. *I smell,* he told himself.

He looked for a side entrance, found one, tested the door. It was open. He went inside. After checking several rooms, he found one with running water and washed himself as best he could.

He walked up a flight of stairs and cautiously approached the large room in which everyone was gathered.

A male was standing in front of everyone. "The message we have is one of Aryan supremacy!" he was saying.

Neshi listened to a little more.

"Ours is a pure white congregation, and we must keep it that way. We must not allow any mixture with other races to creep in. We must keep ourselves spotless before our Lord!"

Perspiration formed in the palms of Neshi's hands.

There were other words, words about burning crosses and hangings and more. Neshi looked at his hands, felt his face, and knew with awful certainty how they would react to him. This was not a place where he could get help.

He could find no other group, no one at all, and he was not surprised that when he returned to the cabin, his new friend was nearly dead.

"What is your name?" the male asked, his voice so low that it was nearly inaudible.

"Neshi."

"A good name. Mine is Matthew, Matthew Rosenberg. They call me a fulfilled Jew."

Matthew—Ma'Tu!

So similar in sound to the nickname Tuati had given him.

Matthew was shivering. "Hold me, Neshi. Please!"

Neshi put his large arms around the other.

"I know what you must have heard," Matthew said. "I

don't blame you for coming back. There was no help to be given. The Lord understands. I understand."

"But you cannot see me, Matthew. You do not know how very different I am. If you could see me, you might feel as they do."

Matthew looked up at him with his sightless eyes. "I cannot see you, my friend, that is true. But even if you were purple skinned, I would thank God for bringing you, ever so briefly, into my life."

"How can you accept God as you do, knowing how He seems to be at the beck and call of those awful ones I heard?"

Matthew's tone was gentle. "Because I know the real Savior, not the one they worship. Their savior is a counterfeit set up by Satan. Those kind aren't believers. They twist the Word to their own purposes."

Matthew still had the Bible in his left hand.

"Take this book," he begged. "Take this wonderful book. It's my gift to you, my brother."

Matthew gasped then, his body becoming limp.

Neshi buried Matthew in back of the cabin, standing by the grave for quite a while. He had known the male for so short a period of time, and yet he felt such loss just then.

He looked at the book that he held in his right hand.

"How could you call me your brother?" he said out loud. "How could you give me a book that meant so much to you?"

He intended to leave then. It was midafternoon, the sky dark with storm clouds. He wanted to get back to the crash site before nighttime. As he started to turn away from the makeshift grave, he hesitated, a streak of cynicism coming to the surface.

What nonsense, he thought, then tossed the book on the ground and walked off.

Less than five minutes later, rain began to fall.

He had an hour's trip to the crash site, and it was only a short distance back to the cabin, where he could dry himself and not risk illness. Dwaun undoubtedly would seek refuge in what was left of the ship. By the time Neshi had made it to the cabin and was inside, the rainfall was torrential.

40

Neshi dozed off briefly and dreamed, not of Etarina or Tuati or Graita, but of Matthew. He dreamed the two of them were sitting by a campfire under a clear sky, and they had been talking for hours.

Matthew read repeatedly from the leather-bound book. The words didn't stay with Neshi upon awakening, but Matthew's manner did—his joy, his utter belief in what was written inside.

"But what of your works?" Neshi remembered saying. "What did you do to earn what you have now?"

Matthew smiled.

The sounds of the storm finally shook Neshi back to reality.

He was shivering.

The Nedians had been convinced that they could not know their God unless they paid for the right through acts they performed on a daily basis. On his own world there was nothing to earn, because there was no God to worship. Or so he had been taught from the cradle onward.

And yet something about Matthew's manner had suggested that he look at this matter of a Creator altogether differently.

"I am cold now," he said. "I am alone. I cannot go to be with my friend as yet. I should never have left him in his grief. I have gone through the reaches of space and landed on dead world after dead world. Now here I am on one with life, and there is still suffering, there is still pain, the future seems cold and bleak. In what do I believe? In whom do I place my trust?"

He looked at several of the other books on the shelf. One in particular caught his attention. He started reading through it.

"But how is it that I understand the language? Why should I be able to read a book when I'm countless millions of miles from home?"

The words were spoken with no hope of response, but he had to say them just the same.

The book was smaller than the leather-bound one. He sat down on the floor and read with fascination.

It was about a female whose family had been confined to places called *concentration camps*, which reminded Neshi of the forced labor farms on his world, where Jerusalemites and others were sent.

She, a brother, and one sister proved to be the only survivors from that family, a large one, indeed.

Afterward, the female was released from the concentration camp. Later, she happened to meet one of the guards, a male who had been particularly cruel.

She knew him instantly. She wanted to slap him, spit at

him, perhaps kick him, but her angry, vengeful thoughts were soon submerged in a flood of forgiveness, no matter how much she initially fought against anything of the kind.

Neshi tried to envision himself ever forgiving those responsible for the torment Etarina had endured.

I cannot! he thought. *How could I be expected to do that?*

And yet this female had lost even more than he had. Still she forgave, it seemed, every act of cruelty, every atrocity committed.

"So different from the attitudes of the Nedians," he said to the emptiness of the cabin. "They had to earn whatever generosity they expected from their God. But the God of this female seems to give away His forgiveness freely."

That was a strange concept to Neshi. Little in his life had been free. He had had to work very hard for everything, including his survival, for longer than he could calculate since the measure of time had been skewed during his travels from galaxy to galaxy.

He read through the rest of the book. The female mentioned something else at one point, something that hit him with immense impact: the Bible. She claimed that reading it changed her life.

Neshi put the book back on the shelf and searched for another copy of the Bible, but the only one was lying on the ground somewhere near Matthew's grave.

He went to the window and looked out at the heavy rain. Then he started pacing the floor. Finally he rushed outside, as though he had no will to do anything but that.

Why am I doing this? he asked himself. *It's nonsense. That absurd little book will be nothing but formless mush by now.*

He approached the site.

The rain was so strong that it had washed away the

layer of soil Neshi had put over the crudely dug grave. Matthew's body was exposed.

Neshi sank to his knees. "No! No!" he screamed. He felt very ill, light-headed. He was close to passing out.

He saw something.

Squinting his eyes in the darkness he—

The Bible!

Lying there, cupped between Matthew's hands.

How could that be?

After picking up the book, he clutched it close to him. Then he jumped to his feet and ran back to the cabin.

41

Nearly morning.

He had slept little, spending the time reading that book, going through various emotional and psychological stages as he did. He bounced from outright rejection and ridicule to grudging interest, back to rejection, then on to skepticism. Finally he just read the book from front to back, absorbing every word, every syllable, every chapter and verse, amazed that nothing had been ruined by the rain except the black leather cover, the pages inside virtually untouched, covered by the man's protective hands.

He spent some time envisioning how that might have happened. He had thrown the book on the ground near Matthew's grave. The rain had started. He hadn't put enough dirt over the body, which had been washed off by the torrent, and Matthew's dead hands had accidentally fallen on the book, covering it, protecting it from being completely ruined.

How logical is that? he thought. *Too coincidental.*

Logic, coincidence, or whatever aside, something had happened, and he was able to hold the book in his hands and read its precious contents.

Precious? he asked himself. *Do I think that?*

Back on his world, he would have incinerated the volume as seditious, and now he was calling it precious!

When he came upon the name *Jerusalem*, he was so startled he had to put the book down. Jerusalem had been a city in turmoil, a city surrounded by its enemies, a city whose citizens were driven to cannibalism, a city conquered by an assaulting horde—just as in his dream!

After all this time, after millions of miles, on this last world of his odyssey, he read of a reality that matched his stark fantasy detail by detail.

If there was that kind of truth in this book, verifying what had been haunting his sleeptime for so long, what else would it contain of equal impact?

It was nearly midday.

Dwaun! He jumped to his feet. *How selfish*, he realized. *He must be frantic, thinking I've been hurt or killed.* He looked at the Bible. *But what wonders I have to tell him!* And so he left the cabin and headed back to the crash site.

Dwaun was cupping his hands in a stream at one end of the little valley when Neshi approached him. Dwaun looked up, scowled, and then returned to what he was doing.

"It has been an extraordinary time," Neshi said, his face flushing red.

"For you, perhaps."

"Forgive me, my friend."

Dwaun stood, hands on his hips, his expression first stern, then becoming a very broad smile. "Of course, Neshi. You are all I have left."

The two of them embraced.

Then both sat by the stream, splashing handfuls of water over their faces.

Finally Neshi picked up the leather-bound book that he had placed to one side and handed it to Dwaun. "Glance through it," he said. "I'll cook us something in the meantime."

He left Dwaun and went to the spot where they had previously made a fire. His friend had been active, trapping several small animals and skinning them. Neshi inspected the bodies and chose one for cooking, falling back on yet another Tekkie skill.

Minutes later, as he was turning the spit over the fire, he wondered how Dwaun would react, supposing that the Nedian would exalt over the truths in that book, that he would be far less reluctant to accept them than Neshi himself had been. Neshi's background had doomed any hope of faith in days gone by, while Dwaun's included absolute faith, albeit that which had to be re-energized and re-earned day after day for the rest of his life.

He was wrong.

Dwaun's instinctive reaction was to reject most of what he read. In fact, he came storming over to Neshi. "Garbage," he said, throwing the book at his friend's feet. "Accept Christ as Savior and Lord! Salvation is by faith plus nothing; it is not of works!" He was pacing angrily. "Pure fantasy," he said. "Pure delusion. At least on Nede we could *pay* for what we got. How can I respect what is supposed to be given freely by God?"

"But that is the wonder of it, Dwaun, the beauty!"

"It is cheap and pointless, a handout to beggars. I refuse to be taken in!"

"But Dwaun, the price has already been paid."

Dwaun looked at him as though Neshi had lost his sanity. "What are you talking about?"

"You spent two hours with the book."

"I did. That's more than enough."

"It's not, Dwaun. I read it for at least ten or twelve hours, page after page."

"What is your point, Neshi?"

"Tuati was willing to sacrifice herself for me, was she not?"

"Yes."

"Christ sacrificed Himself for *us!*"

Dwaun opened his mouth to reply, then stopped. He sat down on a flat rock, as though he had no strength left.

"I believe that, dear, dear friend," Neshi said. "I believe that Tuati and Graita and some of my friends on my home world were given a final chance, were given the Plan, Dwaun. Not the plan of the Natasians or your false god, of Satan himself, but the only Plan that matters for the rest of our lives, Dwaun."

"And having understood truth, they embraced it?" Dwaun asked.

"With mind, body, and soul!"

Dwaun fell backward off the rock and lay there, sobbing.

Neshi crawled over to him.

"My Graita," Dwaun was saying, "my Graita's alive then! She accepted this Christ in time to be—"

"And I pray Etarina as well!" Neshi added.

It was a while before their emotions calmed down, before they could take that leather-bound book and pass it between them, each reading a portion and then handing it to the other, until dusk and beyond. The light of the fire flickered over the thin pages, some of which were streaked with mud but legible. Each word was precious to them, another drop of the purest water their thirsty souls had ever tasted.

"The Bible says that Christ died for *human beings,* Neshi," Dwaun said as they finally lay down on soft moss and looked up at the stars.

"Christ died for *all* His creation," Neshi replied.

"Creatures that do not have a capacity to reason, creatures with no souls, cannot be included because they can never accept or reject," Dwaun mused. "Since you and I can deduce, since we can think and reason, can say yes or no, we must be part of that creation for which Christ gave His life. Is that how we can view the matter?"

"I'm convinced it is indeed, Dwaun. Satan tricked the other Nedians into worshiping a false god of works, not the true God of sacrifice and redemption. They saw part of the truth but not the rest."

The two fell asleep as they talked of such things, Dwaun holding the leather-covered book in his right hand.

Neshi had been puzzled for some time about how Dwaun and he could read and understand that book called the *Holy Bible*. And then he came across a passage that seemed to provide the answer, if only in part:

And suddenly there came a sound from heaven as of a rushing mighty wind, and it filled all the house where they were sitting. And there appeared unto them cloven tongues like as of fire, and it sat upon each of them. And they were all filled with the Holy Ghost, and began to speak with other tongues, as the Spirit gave them utterance.

Acts 2:2–4

That had to be it! He pointed this passage out to Dwaun. "You know, that might be the answer," Dwaun admitted, then noticed another passage. "Here's more, Neshi!"

And there were dwelling at Jerusalem Jews, devout men, out of every nation under heaven. Now when this was noised abroad, the multitude came together, and were confounded, because that every man heard them speak in his own language. And they were all amazed and marvelled, saying one to another, Behold, are not all these which speak Galileans? And how hear we every man in our own tongue, wherein we were born? Parthians, and Medes, and Elamites, and the dwellers in Mesopotamia, and in Judaea, and Cappadocia, in Pontus and Asia, Phrygia, and Pamphylia, in Egypt, and in the parts of Libya about Cyrene, and strangers of Rome, Jews and proselytes, Cretes and Arabians, we do hear them speak in our tongues the wonderful works of God.

Acts 2:5–11

"The wonderful works of God, Neshi!" Dwaun exclaimed. "The mind explodes with the very idea!"

"I talked with Matthew," Neshi recalled, "a stranger, but I understood his words, and he mine."

"And you from another galaxy altogether talked with us!"

They rejoiced throughout the morning, the last morning of their lives.

42

Neshi had been away from camp, fishing in a lake a mile or two south. He had caught some hearty-looking species and was walking back to camp when he heard a scream.

Dwaun!

He dropped his catch and ran ahead, tripping once and spraining his ankle. He had to limp the rest of the way.

Dwaun was standing near Graita's grave, his back to Neshi.

"I heard you scream," Neshi said at the top of his voice.

Dwaun turned, the front of his chest covered with blood. "Those who attacked your friend Matthew, they must have—" He fell forward, across the grave.

Neshi ran to his side.

"Imagine, my dearest friend," Dwaun said weakly. "Across dead galaxies to my own death on an unknown world!" He attempted to laugh ironically but coughed instead, pain racking his body. And then suddenly the frown disappeared, the eyes widened. "Neshi, it's all true, my alien brother. The others weren't deceived."

He reached up and placed his hand on Neshi's shoulder. "An angel is reaching down to me now. And by his side is Someone in shining raiment. Oh, Neshi, it—" And then he was gone.

Neshi hugged his body for many minutes. There was no way to track the time, but it was a very long period, because Neshi was reluctant to assign another comrade to the emptiness of space or the cold earth.

Later, he buried Dwaun in the same grave as Graita and piled dirt back on slowly, his tears mixing with the soil. Then he stood, unable to leave, and let out a cry of utter despair.

"Lord!" he called, "I have no one left. *I am alone!*"

Where could he go? Into that small town and listen to sermons of Aryan hatred in a congregation of men with shaven heads? Or past it, to whatever lay beyond on this strange world?

"But at least there is *life*," he said to the loneliness. "There are no shells of doomed civilizations, the remains of what was." Then a notion hit him. He sat down on the ground, looking through the leather-bound book, reading of the decadence of the city of Jerusalem before it was overrun and the prophecies in the last section of the book promising tribulation, beasts, and a great whore.

This planet's future was to be like the others. It was just that this time he had gotten there earlier, before the decay had spread throughout, before the final judgment. Some would survive, he knew. Some would be taken at the Second Coming and join the Savior forever and ever. But the rest would remain in frightful allegiance to the Prince of Darkness.

"BEHOLD, THE MAESTRO OF HELL COMES FORTH TO CLAIM YOU FOREVER!"

That chilling voice remained in his recollection, burrowed deep, unquenched.

He bowed his head in prayer, awkward prayer, the prayer of a new babe. "But the devil has no claim on me any longer, Lord," he said with gathering triumph. "Nor on Dwaun, Tuati, or Graita. We have faced the truth, and the truth has saved us."

He never heard the two big males with rifles and knives come up behind him, never felt the blade enter his back the second or third time, never sensed his body touching the earth. All he heard was a single voice—familiar, soft—saying a single time, "Baba!"

43

The skinheads uncovered the grave, pulled out the other bodies, dumped all three in the rear of a pickup truck, and took them back to town. People were amazed and puzzled. None had the anthropological training to do much but gawk, though.

"Weird," one of them said. "We can't tell anyone about this. Might bring too much attention to our little community."

The rest agreed, and so nothing more was done, except to use the bodies in various ways: the skin for a couple of lampshades, some necklaces out of the spines; the hands, preserved, were bookends anchored in clear crystal bases.

The leftover bits and pieces were dumped into a hole and disinfectant poured over. The bones, soon dissolved, flowed into the soil.

There was laughter over what had happened, and in the midst of the cigarette smoke and booze, someone talked about the good old days of burning crosses.

Epilogue

"So sad, Storyteller," a listener remarked, "and yet so beautiful."

"You are correct, my friend," Storyteller replied. "Beauty arising from the ashes, into eternity."

"Some questions remain unanswered," another listener pointed out. "For example: Where did the colonists who landed on each of the different worlds come from? Or was it that Neshi's planet and Nede were exceptions in that life began on the rest through divine acts of creation, just as on Earth?"

Storyteller waited, knowing there would be more.

"Who, really, was this Smythe character?" the other continued. "Mind you, Storyteller, these are only three of a number of questions. When will you enlighten us?"

"Wait?" a third listener exclaimed. "I have a question, too: Is this tale just that, a parable perhaps, a fable? Does a being named Neshi exist? And others who are called Dwaun, Tuati, and Graita?"

"And Etarina?" Storyteller added. "Surely she should not be omitted from your list?"

"Yes! Etarina, to be sure."

Storyteller would not be hurried, looking teasingly at the gathered multitude.

Finally he said, slowly, "All that you ask of me truly belongs to a second tale of wonder and adventure."

"When?" they asked. "Tell us when that tale will be told to the delight of all."

"Soon, friends! Soon indeed. We do have eternity ahead of us. After all, since time no longer exists, we can hardly run out of it. I promise you this: Ultimately you will know all the answers—and you will rejoice over them, you will!"

Storyteller said nothing further but closed up his parchments and signaled that the encounter was at an end.

One of those listening was a bit impetuous, not really expecting any response but still prodded by some flash of intuition. As Storyteller was leaving, the impetuous one stood and shouted after him, "Say hello to Etarina for us!"

Storyteller hesitated momentarily, his head turned in profile, his smile barely visible. Then he walked down the street of gold, humming.